Accounting English
會計英語（雙語教材）

主　编○陽春暉
副主编○吴　丹　朱　懿

前　言

伴隨著世界經濟一體化的步伐以及《企業會計準則》廣泛實施，會計不僅在制度和理論上，更是在實務中，與國際會計實現了實質性的趨同。世界越融合，對國際化人才的需求就越強烈，尤其是既有專業知識，又能熟練使用英語的人才，具有廣泛的社會需求性和發展空間。一本好的專業英語教材無疑會幫助會計專業學生和其他會計從業人員更好地掌握"專業+英語"的相關知識。本書正是本着滿足社會需求的原則，爲廣大的會計專業學生和會計從業人員以及從商者編寫的會計英語教材。

作爲會計專業英語課程的入門教材，本書具有如下特點：

1. 體系完整、結構合理

本書是會計專業英語系列教材之一，主要以基礎會計爲體系，内容包括會計的基礎理論、平衡原理、會計核算體系、核算方法以及會計報表等。爲各類初學會計的讀者提供了最基礎的會計知識。

2. 源於教學實踐、針對性强

本書源於老師們十多年來會計專業英語教學的積累，在沿用傳統會計學的體系模式的同時，充分吸收了當代西方會計的理論與實務方法，去粗取精，中西結合，以較新的内容呈現給學生，使之更具現實性、國際化，以順應會計國際化的發展趨勢。

3. 內容充實、難易適中

本書內容完整,英文習題豐富齊全。課文行文地道、純正、專業,既重視會計基礎概念的通俗易懂又強調會計核算原理的實際應用。選用典型的案例,思路清晰,便於理解。每章後面都配有大量的相關練習題,難度適宜,可幫助讀者鞏固已學的內容,有助於提高讀者的會計英語閱讀理解能力與實務操作能力。

4. 適用對象廣泛

本書不僅可用作大學院校會計學專業的大學生專業英語教學和雙語教學的理想教材,也可用作其他會計從業人員、教學人員、管理人員等的閱讀材料。 本書向讀者提供了豐富的會計專業英語資料,是一本實用性較強的教學和自學用書。

本書由陽春暉主編,負責構思全書框架結構、制定編排目錄章節、編寫部分內容及統稿總纂,副主編爲朱懿、吳丹。另外,參加本書編寫工作的還有池昭梅、鄧德宏和秦弋雯幾位老師。本書的出版是一個階段工作的總結和匯報,又是一個新的開始,我們期盼讀者的意見和建議,以期改進。

編 者

Contents

Chapter 1 Introduction to Accounting 1
   Unit 1   An Overview of Accounting   1
   Unit 2   Types of Business   3
   Unit 3   The Users of Financial Information   6
   Unit 4   The Regulatory Framework   9
   Key Terms   12
   Multiple Choice Questions   13
   Exercises   15

Chapter 2 The Basic Concepts of Accounting 16
   Unit 1   Fundamental Accounting Assumptions   16
   Unit 2   The Qualitative Characteristics of Financial Information   18
   Key Terms   23
   Multiple Choice Questions   24
   Exercises   25

Chapter 3 Double Entry Method of Accounting 26
   Unit 1   Accounting Elements and Accounting Equation   26
   Unit 2   Double Entry Bookkeeping   30
   Unit 3   The Use of Double Entry Bookkeeping   33
   Key Terms   37
   Multiple Choice Questions   38

Exercises   39

Chapter 4   Accounting Procedures Ⅰ: Journalizing   42

Unit 1   Types of Business Documentation   43

Unit 2   Books of Prime Entry   51

Key Terms   56

Multiple Choice Questions   56

Exercises   58

Chapter 5   Accounting Procedures Ⅱ: Posting   59

Unit 1   Ledger   59

Unit 2   Control Accounts   62

Key Terms   70

Multiple Choice Questions   71

Exercises   72

Chapter 6   Accounting Procedures Ⅲ: Closing and Adjusting   74

Unit 1   Trial Balance   74

Unit 2   Error Correction   80

Unit 3   Adjustments   87

Key Terms   106

Multiple Choice Questions   106

Exercises   112

Chapter 7   Financial Statements   114

Unit 1   Statement of Financial Position   114

Unit 2   Income Statement   118

Unit 3   Statement of Cash Flows   119

Contents

Key Terms 124

Multiple Choice Questions 125

Exercises 128

Chapter 8 Recording Transactions 130

Unit 1 Recording Credit Transactions 130

Unit 2 Recording Cash Transactions 141

Unit 3 Fulfilling an Accounting Cycle 147

Key Terms 157

Multiple Choice Questions 157

Exercises 161

Bibliography 163

Chapter 1
Introduction to Accounting

Accounting is vital to a strong company, keeping track of the business's finances and its continued profitability. Without accounting, a business owner would not know how much money were coming in or going out, or how to plan for the future. The actions taken by accounting professionals—from bookkeepers to certified public accountants (CPAs)—make it possible to monitor the company's financial status and provide reports and projections that affect the organization's decisions.

Unit 1 An Overview of Accounting

1.1 Induction to Accounting

Accounting is an information system that identifies, records, and communicates relevant, reliable, and comparable information about an organisation's business activities that can be transactions and events relevant to an organisation. Recording business activities requires keeping a chronological log of transactions and events measured in monetary unit, and classified and summarised in a useful format. Communication business activities requires preparing accounting reports, such as financial statements. It also requires analyzing and interpreting such reports.

Accounting is often called the language of business because all organisations set up an accounting information system to communicate data to help people make better decisions. It records the past growth or decline of the business. Careful analysis of these results and trends may suggest the ways in which the business may grow in the future. Expansion or reorganisation should not be planned without the proper analysis of the accounting information; selling a new product and the campaign advertising should not be launched without the help of accounting expertise. Accounting information affects many aspects of our lives. When we earn money, pay taxes, invest savings, budget earnings, and plan for the future, we are influenced by accounting.

1.2 The Purpose of Financial Reporting

The accounting system of a business records and summarises the financial performance/position of a business at a certain period of time. This information is crucial to various stakeholders of the business who will analyse this information to make significant economic decisions. It is vital importance that these stakeholders have good quality information to be able to make good quality decisions.

First, this information is recorded in books of prime entry.

Then, this information is analysed in the books of prime entry and the totals are posted to the ledger accounts.

Finally, this information is summarised in the financial statements.

1.3 Financial Accounting and Management Accounting

1.3.1 Financial Accounting

Financial accounting is mainly a method of reporting the results and financial position of a business. It is not primarily concerned with providing information towards the more efficient running of the business. Although financial accounts are of interest to management, their principal function is to satisfy the information needs of persons not involved in running the business. They provide historical information.

1.3.2 Management Accounting

Management (or cost) accounting is a management information system which analyses data to provide information as a basis for managerial action. A management accountant is to present accounting information in the form which is helpful to management.

The information needs of management go far beyond those of other account users. Managers have the responsibility of planning and controlling the resources of the business so they need much more detailed information, thus management accounting is an integral part of management activity concerned with identifying, presenting and interpreting information used for:

- formulating strategy;
- planning and controlling activities;
- decision making;
- optimising the use of resources.

Unit 2　Types of Business

Businesses range enormously in size, from large oil companies, mobile telephone operators and big supermarket chains down to small one-person operations, such as a plumber, a window cleaner. They all have something in common. They sell goods or services for money.

Most type of business can be classified in terms of who is involved in them and how the organisations operate.

2.1　Sole Trader/Proprietorship

An individual can run his or her own business, either alone as a one-person operation or as a business owner with several employees. The owner is entitled to all the profits (that is what is left after expenses have been deducted from income) and suffers all the losses made by the business.

A sole trader may be involved in:

- Manufacturing: making something from raw materials, for example, furniture.

· Trading: buying and selling goods in a small shop.

· Service: providing a service for customers, such as hairdressing.

Accounting conventions recognise the business as a separate entity from its owner. However, legally, the business and personal affairs of a sole trader are not distinguished in any way. The most important consequences of this is that a sole trader has complete personal unlimited liability. Business debts which cannot be paid from business assets must be met for sale of personal assets, such as a house or a car.

The advantages of operating as a sole trader include flexibility and autonomy. A sole trader can manage the business as he or she likes and can introduce or withdraw capital at any time.

2.2 Partnership

Two or more people working together with the idea of generating a profit from a business are known as partners. Although governed by law, partnerships known as legally as firms, can be quite informal. The partners agree how the firm should be run, partners share profits and losses in accordance with their agreement.

Like sole trader, a partnership is not legally distinguished from its members. Personal assets of the partners may have to be used to pay the debts of the partnership business.

The mainly advantages of trading as a partnership is that there are many owners rather than one. It means that:

· More resources may be available, including capital, specialist knowledge, skills and ideas.

· Administrative expenses for a partnership may be lower than the equivalent number of sole traders, due to economics of scale.

· Partners can substitute for each other.

· Partners must introduce or withdraw capital with providing arguments of all the partners.

2.3 Companies

Unlike sole traders and partnerships, companies are established as separate legal entities to their owners. This is achieved through the process of incorporation. The owners of the company invest capital in the business in return for a shareholding that is a share of the residual assets of the business (i.e., what is left when the business winds up). The shareholders are not personally liable for the debts of the company and whilst they may lose their investment if the company becomes insolvent but they will not have to pay the outstanding debts of the company if such a circumstance arises. Likewise, the company is not affected by the insolvency (or death) of individual shareholders.

2.4 Comparison of Companies to Sole Traders and Partnerships

The fact that a company is a separate legal entity means that it is very different from a sole trader or partnership in a number of ways.

(1) Property holding.

The property of a limited company belongs to the company. A change in the ownership of shares in the company will have no effect on the ownership of the company's property. However, in a partnership, the firm's property belongs directly to the partners who can take it with them if they leave the partnership.

(2) Transferable shares.

Shares in a limited company can usually be transferred without the consent of the other shareholders. In the absence of agreement to the contrary, a new partner cannot be introduced into a firm without the consent of all existing partners.

(3) Suing and being sued.

As a separate legal person, a limited company can sue and be sued in its own name. Judgments relating to companies do not affect the members personally.

(4) Security for loans.

A company has greater scope for raising loans and may secure them with floating charges. A floating charge is a mortgage over the constantly fluctuation assets of a company providing security for the lender of money to a company. It dose not prevent the company dealing with the assets in the ordinary course of business. Such a charge is useful when a company has not non-current assets, such as land, but does have large and valuable inventories.

Generally, the law does not permit partnerships or individuals to secure loans with a floating charge.

(5) Taxation.

Because a company is legally separated from its shareholders, it is taxed separately from its shareholders. Partners and sole traders are personally liable for income tax on the profits made by their business.

Unit 3 The Users of Financial Information

3.1 The Need for Financial Statements

There are various groups of people who need information about the activities of a business. Why do businesses need to produce financial statements? If a business is being run efficiently, why should it have to go through all the bother of accounting procedures in order to produce financial information?

The International Accounting Standards Board states in its document (*Framework for the preparation and presentation of financial statements*) that 'the objective of financial statements is to provide information about the financial position, performance and changes in financial position of an entity that is useful to a wide range of users in making economic decisions.'

In other words, a business should produce information about its activities be-

Chapter 1　Introduction to Accounting

cause there are various groups of people who want or need to know that information. This sounds rather vague. To make it clearer, we will study the classes of people who need information about a business. We also need to think about what information in particular is of interest to the members of each class.

3.2　Users of Financial Statements and Accounting Information

The following people are likely to be interested in financial information about a large company with listed shares.

(1) Managers of the company.

Who appointed by the company's owners to supervise the day-to-day activities of the company. They need information about the company's financial situation as it is currently and as it is expected to be in the future. This is to enable them to manage the business efficiently and to make effective decisions.

(2) Shareholders of the company.

For example, the company's owners want to assess how well the management is performing. They want to know how profitable the company's operations are and how much profit they can afford to withdraw from the business for their own use.

(3) Trade contacts.

Suppliers who provide goods to the company on credit want to know the company's ability to pay its debts; customers who purchase the goods or services provided by the company need to know that the company is a secure source of supply and is in no danger of having to close down.

(4) Investors and creditors.

Investors and creditors provide the money a business need to get started. When a company opened its first store, the company had no track record. To decide whether to help start a new venture, potential investors evaluate how many income they can expect on their investment. This means analysing the financial statements of the business. Before deciding to invest in a company, you may examine the company's financial statements. Before making a loan to the company, banks should evaluate the company's ability to meet scheduled payment.

(5) The taxation authorities.

The taxation authorities want to know about business profits in order to assess the tax payable by the company, including sales taxes.

(6) Employees of the company.

Empolyees should have a right to know information about the company's financial situation, because their future careers and the size of their wages and salaries depend on it.

(7) Financial analysts and advisers.

They need information for their clients or audience. For example, stockbrokers need information to advise investors; credit agencies want information to advise potential suppliers of goods to the company; journalists need information for their reading public.

(8) Government and their agencies.

They are interested in the allocation of resources and the activities of business entities. They also require information in order to provide a basis for national statistics.

(9) The public.

Entities affect members of the public in a variety of ways. For example, they may make a substantial contribution to a local economy by providing employment and using local suppliers.

(10) Other users.

For example, labour unions demand wages that come from the employer's reported income. Another important factor is the effect of an entity on the environment, for example as regards pollution.

Accounting information is summarised in financial statements to satisfy the information needs of different groups. However, not all will be equally satisfied.

Chapter 1　Introduction to Accounting

Unit 4　The Regulatory Framework

4.1　The Framework

One of the most important documents that underpinning the preparation of financial statements is the Conceptual Framework for Financial Reporting (the Framework), which was prepared by the IASB.

The framework presents the main ideas, concepts and principles upon which all International Financial Reporting Standards, and therefore financial statements, are based. It includes discussion of:

- the objectives of financial reporting;
- the qualitative characteristics of useful financial information;
- the definition, recognition and measurement of the elements from which the financial statements are constructed;
- the concepts of accruals and going concern;
- the concepts of capital and capital maintenance.

4.2　International Financial Reporting Standards (IFRS)

Due to the increasingly global nature of investment and business operation there has been a move towards the 'internationalization' of financial reporting. This 'harmonisation' was considered necessary to provide consistent and comparable information to an increasingly global audience. Prior to 2003, accounting standards were issued as International Accounting Standards(IASs). In 2003, IFRS 1 was issued and all new standards are now designated as IFRSs.

IFRS are not enforceable in any country. As we will see shortly, they are developed by an international organisation that has no international authority. To become enforceable they must be adopted by a country's national financial reporting standard setter.

Within the European Union, IFRS were adopted for all listed entities in 2005. Other countries have adopted IFRS include: Argentina, Australia, Brazil, Canada, Russia, Mexico, Saudi Arabia and South Africa. The US, China and India are going through a process of 'covergence', whereby they are updating their national standards over time so that they are consistent with IFRS.

4.3 Structure of the IFRS Regulatory System

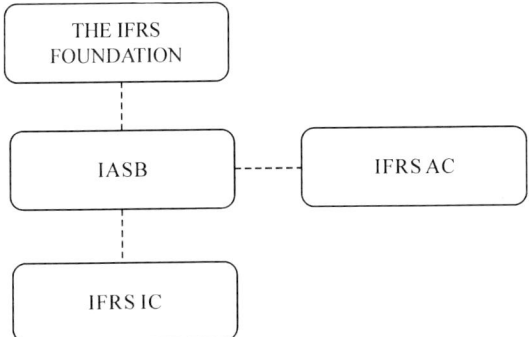

Figure 1.1 Structure of the IFRS Regulatory System

4.3.1 International Financial Reporting Standards(IFRS) Foundation

The IFRS Foundation [formerly known as the International Accounting Standards Committee Foundation(IASC)] is the supervisory body for the IASB(International Accounting Standards Board), and is responsible for governance issues and ensuring each member body is properly funded.

The principal objectives of the IFRS Foundation are to:

· develop a set of high quality, understandable, enforceable and globally accepted financial reporting standards;

· promote the use and rigorous application of those standards;

· to take account of the financial reporting needs of emerging economies and small and medium sized entities;

· bring about the convergence of national and international financial reporting standards.

4.3.2 *International Accounting Standards Board (IASB)*

The IASB is the independent standard setting body of the IFRS foundation. Its members are responsible for the development and publication of IFRSs, and interpretations developed by the IFRS IC. Upon its creation the IASB also adopted all existing International Accounting Standards.

All of the most important national standard setters are represented on the IASB and their views are taken into account so that a consensus can be reached. All national standard setters can issue IASB discussion papers and exposure drafts for comment in their own countries, so that the views of all preparers and users of financial statements can be represented. Each major national standard setter 'leads' certain international standard-setting projects.

4.3.3 *The IFRS Interpretations Committee (IFRS IC)*

The IFRS IC reviews widespread accounting issues (in the context of IFRS) on a timely basis and provides authoritative guidance on these issues (IFRICs). Their meetings are open to the public that is similar to the IASB and they work closely with national standard setters.

4.3.4 *The IFRS Advisory Council (IFRS AC)*

The IFRS AC is the formal advisory body to the IASB and the IFRS Foundation. It is comprised of a wide range of members who are affected by the IASB's work. Their objectives include:

· Advising the IASB on agenda decisions and priorities in their work.

· Informing the IASB of the views of the council with regard to major standard setting projects.

· Giving other advice to the IASB or to the trustees.

4.4 Development of an IFRS

The procedure for the development of an IFRS is as follows:

· The IASB identifies a subject and appoints an advisory committee to advise on the issues.

· The IASB publishes an exposure draft for public comment, being a draft version of the intended standard.

· Following the consideration of comments received on the draft, the IASB publishes the final text of the IFRS.

· At any stage the IASB may issue a discussion paper to encourage comment.

· The publication of an IFRS, exposure draft or IFRIC interpretation requires the votes of at least eight of the 15 IASB members.

Key Terms

financial reporting	財務報告
financial data	財務數據
financial statements	財務報表
financial accounting	財務會計
management accounting	管理會計
financial position	財務狀況
sole trader	獨資企業
partnership	合夥企業
company	公司
manager	管理層
shareholder	股東
investor	投資者
creditor	債權人

Chapter 1 Introduction to Accounting

supplier	供貨商
customer	客戶
the taxation authorities	稅務部門
financial analyst	財務分析師
regulatory framework	規則框架

International Financial Reporting Standards (IFRSs)
國際財務報告準則

International Accounting Standards Board (IASB)
國際會計準則委員會

IFRS Advisory Council (IFRS AC)
國際財務報告準則諮詢委員會

IFRS Interpretations Committee (IFRS IC)
國際財務報告準則解釋委員會

IFRS Foundation
國際財務報告準則基金會

Multiple Choice Questions

1. Purposes of an accounting system include all of the following except ( ).
    A. interpret and record the effects of business transactions
    B. classify the effects of transactions to facilitate the preparation of reports
    C. dictate the specific types of business transactions that the enterprise may engage in
    D. summarize and communicate information to decision makers

2. Which of the following statements is true? ( ).
    A. The directors of a company are liable for any losses of the company
    B. Sole trader business is owned by shareholders and operated by the proprietor
    C. Partners are liable for losses in a partnership in proportion to their profit

share ratio

D. A company is run by directors on behalf of its shareholders

3. Which of the following statements is particularly useful for managers? (   ).

  A. Financial statements for the last financial year

  B. Tax records for the past five years

  C. Budgets for the coming financial year

  D. Bank statements for the past year

4. Which one of the following is the main aim of accounting? (   ).

  A. To maintain ledger accounts for every asset and liability

  B. To provide financial information to users of such information

  C. To produce a trial balance

  D. To record every financial transaction individually

5. Which of the following user groups requires the most detailed financial information? (   ).

  A. The management

  B. Investors and potential investors

  C. Government agencies

  D. Employees

6. Which of the following statements are true? (   ).

(1) Accounting can be described as the recording and summarising of transactions.

(2) financial accounting describes the production of a statement of financial position and statement of profit or loss for internal use.

  A. (1) only   B. (2) only

  C. Both (1) and (2)   D. None

7. Which one of the following statements is true in relation to a partnership? (   ).

Chapter 1 Introduction to Accounting

　　A. A partnership is a separate legal entity

　　B. A partnership is jointly owned and managed by the partners

　　C. A partnership can raise capital by issuing shares to members of the public

　　D. A partnership is able to own property and other assets in its own name

8. Which one of the following statements is true in relation to a sole trader? (　).

　　A. A sole trader cannot have any employees

　　B. A sole trader is able to introduce or withdraw capital from the business at any time

　　C. A sole trader has limited liability for the debts of the business

　　D. A sole trader can operate a business from only one location

9. Which one of the following statements is true in relation to a limited liability company? (　).

　　A. A limited liability company can incur liabilities in its own name

　　B. A limited liability company cannot acquire assets in its own name

　　C. A limited liability company cannot incur liabilities in its own name

　　D. A limited liability company can be formed on an informal basis by simple agreement between the first shareholders

Exercises

1. It is easy to see how 'internal' people get hold of accounting information. A manager, for example, can just go along to the accounts department and ask the staff there to prepare whatever accounting statements he needs. But external users of accounts cannot do this. How, in practice, can a business contact or a financial analyst access accounting information about a company?

2. What is the fundamental objective of financial reporting?

3. Identify seven user groups who need accounting information.

Chapter 2
The Basic Concepts of Accounting

Accounting practice has developed gradually over time. Many of its procedures are operated automatically by people who have never questioned whether alternative of certain concepts which are by no means self-evidence; nor are they the only possible concepts which could be used to build up an accounting framework. In this chapter we shall single out the important assumptions and concepts for discussion.

Unit 1 Fundamental Accounting Assumptions

The IASB's Framework that a conceptual framework on which IFRSs are based, sets out two important underlying assumptions for financial statements, the Going concern and the Accruals Basis.

1.1 Going Concern

The financial statements are prepared on the assumption that the entity will continue to be in operation for the foreseeable future. In other words, the entity has no intention to liquidate or reduce the size of its operations. If the concept is not applicable then the entity will not use the historical cost principle. As a going concern, the entity will show its assets in the statement of financial position at historical cost, as the entity will be in existence over the remaining life of the assets. Correspondingly, debtors are shown on the statement of financial position at the amount receivable in the ordinary course of business. If the entity is no more a going concern, then the assets will be shown at the realisable value or break-up value.

Chapter 2 The Basic Concepts of Accounting

For example, a retailer commences business on 1 January and buys inventory of 100 T-shirts, each costing $ 10. During the year he sells 70 T-shirts at $ 20 each. If the business is regarded as a going concern, the inventory unsold at 31 December will be carried forward into the following year, when the cost of the remaining T-shirts will be matched against the eventual sale proceeds in computing that year's profits, the thirty T-shirts will therefore be valued at $ 300 (30 × $ 10). In another situation, if the business is to be closed down and the remaining T-shirts will realise only $ 15 each in a forced sale, the remaining thirty T-shirts must be valued at the amount they will realise in a forced sale, for $ 450 (30 × $ 15)

1.2 Accrual Basis

Under the accrual basis, transactions and events are recognised when they occur and are recorded or reported in the financial statements in the period to which they relate irrespective of whether cash was received or paid. Revenue and costs (expenses) are accrued as they are earned or incurred. Accrual basis accounting is complex and complete. It records all cash transactions, including collecting from customers; receiving cash from interest earned; borrowing money; paying off loans; issuing stock; paying salaries, rent, income tax, and other expenses. It also records such non-cash transactions as purchase on credit; sales on credit; depreciation expense; accrual of interest and other expenses incurred but not yet paid; usage of prepaid insurance, supplies, and other prepaid expenses.

In the context of revenue, the concept used is the realisation concept. For example, if an enterprise sells some goods on credit, the sale is immediately recorded and an asset receivable will be recorded even though the customer has not yet paid for the goods. If the goods were delivered on 18 June and the payment was made on 20 June, the sale is deemed to have take place on 18 June.

Expenses are also recognised when they occur but not when money is paid. For example, utility bills for the month of December (year end at 31 December) will be taken in as expenses of the current month/year and a liability for the expenses will be recorded even though the bills will be settled in the following year. This is termed as accrued expenses. In contrast, sometimes payments may be made in advance, for example insurance premium for 18 months is paid on 1 January year 1. At the end of year 1, the amount taken in as insurance expense for year 1 will be for 12 months and the six months for year 2 will be treated as prepaid expenses.

At the same time, the income for the year is matched with the expenses incurred in earning that income. Out of the principle of accrual comes the matching concept. The concept refers to the measurement of profit where costs/expenses is set against the revenue that the expenses generated. Sales for the period are offset with the costs of the inventory sold. An example is the provision and charging for depreciation over the economic life of the assets.

Unit 2　The Qualitative Characteristics of Financial Information

Qualitative characteristics are the attributes that make information provided in financial statements useful to others. The Framework splits qualitative characteristics into two categories:

(1) Fundamental qualitative characteristics.
- Relevance
- Reliability

(2) Enhancing qualitative characteristics.
- Comparability
- Verifiability
- Timeliness
- Understandability

Chapter 2 The Basic Concepts of Accounting

2.1 Fundamental Qualitative Characteristics

2.1.1 Relevance

Only relevant information can be useful. Information is relevance if it has the ability to influence the economic decisions of users, and is provided in time to influence those decisions. Information that is relevant has predictive and confirmatory value. Predictive value enables users to evaluate or assess past, present or future events. Confirmatory value helps users to confirm or corrects past evaluations and assessments.

The relevance of information is affected by its nature and materiality. Materiality is an entity specific aspect of relevance and depends on the size of the item or error judged in the particular circumstances of its omission or misstatement. Although an item may not seem material, its inclusion or omission may influence the judgment of the user of financial information. For example, if an entity with millions of ringgit of assets buys a water dispenser costing $ 1 000 which can be used for five years, it may decide to write it off as an expense. To a small enterprise, that purchase may be recorded as an asset.

2.1.2 Reliability

Financial information is reliable if it is free from error and bias, and represents faithfully the events and transactions that have occurred. To be a perfectly faithful representation, financial information would possess the following characteristics:

(1) Completeness.

Information in the financial statements has to be complete; otherwise it will not be reliable and relevant. Omission of information may render the information presented false or misleading.

(2) Neutrality.

Information contained in the financial statements is to be free from bias (deliberate or systematic) and should not be governed by economic consequence of the reporting entity. Neutrality is lost if the financial statements are prepared so as to influence the user to make a judgment or decision in order to achieve a predetermined outcome.

(3) Free from error.

Information must be free from error within the bounds of materiality. A material error or an omission can cause the financial statements to be false or misleading and thus unreliable and deficient in terms of their relevance. Free from error does not mean perfectly accurate in all respects. For example, where an estimate has been used the amount must be described clearly and accurately as being estimate.

(4) Prudence.

Prudence requires preparers of financial information to be cautious in the exercise of judgment to ensure that income and assets are not overstated, and expenses and liabilities are not understated. Out of this comes the rules such as recognising gains and income only when realised; recognising immediately losses that seem probable.

For example, if the net realisable value of inventory falls below cost, the loss is recognised immediately in that the inventory will be valued at the lower value. On the other hand, if inventory's selling price increases, the gain is recognised only when the inventory is sold and the inventory is valued at cost. Another example is the practice of providing for doubtful debts.

2.2 Enhancing Qualitative Characteristics

2.2.1 Comparability

In order to make decisions, users need to compare information between entities and over a time period. The information from different entities is comparable if there is consistency in the accounting treatment of the economic events and transactions over time, and in the disclosure of accounting policies.

An important implication of comparability is that users are informed of the accounting policies employed in preparation of the financial statements, any changes in those policies and the effects of such changes. Compliance with accounting standards, including the disclosure of the accounting policies used by the entity, helps to achieve comparability.

2.2.2 Verifiability

Verifiability can be direct or indirect. Direct verifiability means verifying amount or other representation through direct observation, such as counting cash. Indirect verification means checking the inputs to a model, formula or other technique and recalculating the outputs using the same methodology.

2.2.3 Timeliness

Timeliness means having information available to decision makers in time to be capable of influencing their decisions. Generally, the older information is becoming less useful. If there is delay in supplying the the information, the information may be relevant in a limited manner even though it may be reliable. Therefore, entities have to find a balance between providing timely information which is relevant and reliable. More of one may mean less of the other.

2.2.4 Understandability

There are many different users and decisions makers. The level of accounting, business knowledge they possess, the methods of decision-making they employ, the ability to process the information, the information they already possess and their ability to obtain additional information differ among various decision makers. It is assumed that users of financial information have a reasonable knowledge of business, accounting and economic activities, and with due diligence, will be able to analyse the information provided.

2.3 Other Important Accounting Concepts

There are a number of other accounting concepts that underpin the preparation of financial statements. The most significant ones include as follows.

2.3.1 Substance over Form

Transactions and events are to be reported as to the commercial or economic reality and not strictly according to legal form. The substance of a transaction may not be consistent with that suggested by its legal form so the transaction or event has to be examined in whole along with its related transactions.

For example, where assets are acquired through hire-purchase, the legal title stays with the seller and only passes to the customer when all the hire-purchase payments have been made. Therefore, it may appear that the asset should appear in the account of the seller as the seller has legal title. The substance of the transaction is that the control and benefits attached to the asset are with the customer. Therefore, the commercial substance is that the asset will be reported in the accounts of the customer. The amount owed on the capital sum to the seller will be treated as a liability. Another example is when an entity contracts to lease motor vehicles with the option to purchase it. Though it may appear as a rental of motor vehicles, it is in fact acquiring 'beneficial ownership' and not legal ownership at the beginning of the lease contract. Therefore, the motor vehicles are considered to be the assets of the entity (lessee).

2.3.2 Consistency

It is assumed that the enterprise will apply the same accounting treatment and policies for similar transactions or events, and these policies and principles will be adopted from year to year. For example, if the entity depreciates a building using the straight-line method; then all similar buildings will also be depreciated using the straight-line method. The same depreciation method is used from one accounting year to another. Application of consistency allows financial statements to be comparable.

2.3.3 The Business Entity Concept

This principle means that the financial accounting information presented in the financial statements relates only to the activities of the business and not to those of the owner. From an accounting perspective the business is treated as being separate from its owners.

2.4 Constraints on Relevant and Reliable Information

At times, there might be more of relevance than reliability, and vice versa. For example, if financial statements were delayed until all the future events that affect them were to come to pass, they would be far more reliable. Uncollectable accounts, warranty reserves, and useful lives of depreciable assets would not have to be estimated. On the other hand, the timeliness of the financial statements would suffer, and thus the statements would lack relevance. Therefore, a degree of reliability is sacrificed to gain relevance. The relative importance of the characteristics changes from situation to situation and call for the exercise of professional judgment.

Key Terms

accounting assumptions	會計假設
going concern	持續經營
accrual basis	權責發生制
relevance	相關性
reliability	可靠性
comparability	可比性
timeliness	及時性
understandability	可理解性
materiality	重要性
completeness	完整性
neutrality	中立性
free from error	準確性

prudence	謹慎性
substance over form	實質重於形式
consistency	一致性
the business entity concept	會計主體

Multiple Choice Questions

1. Which of the following accounting assumptions or principles is concerned when we ask the question "will the business enterprise remain in operation for the foreseeable future in the same line of industry"? (   ).

    A. Going concern   B. Reliability

    C. Materiality   D. Relevance

2. Reliability means that (   ).

    A. a company uses the same accounting principles from year to year

    B. the information has feedback value

    C. the information is a faithful representation of what it purports to be

    D. accounting information can be compared with other enterprises in the industry

3. Chenghe Company purchased a ruler for $2.00. The ruler is expected to last for ten years. Tony, the accountant, expensed the cost of the ruler in the year of the purchase. Which constrain has Tony taken into account when making his accounting decision? (   ).

    A. Prudence   B. Neutrality

    C. Relevance   D. Materiality

4. If the going concern assumption is no longer valid for a company, (   ).

    A. land held as an investment would be valued at its liquidation value

    B. all prepaid assets would be completely written off immediately

    C. total contributed capital and retained earnings would remain unchanged

D. the allowance for uncollectible accounts would be eliminated

Exercises

Identify which assumption, characteristic, or concept best describes the following:

1. PQR Company reports revenue when it is earned instead of when the cash is received.

2. ACE Company writes down its stock of finished goods to the estimated selling price when the selling prices of the goods fall below the cost.

3. En Samad ensures that personal and business record keepings are kept separate.

4. NNN Company sold a plant to Lease Company and immediately leased it back for the remaining life of the asset. NNN Company still has the asset in its account.

5. Mickey Company depreciates all it motor vehicles using the reducing balance methods.

6. Snow White Company provides for all specific doubtful debts when finalising its annual financial statements.

7. The Dwarf Company bought a machine under hire-purchase agreement and records it as its asset shows the amount owing on the capital sum to seller as its liability even though the legal title to the machine is with the seller.

8. Minnie Company paid for insurance expenses for 18 months of $ 9,000 butrecognises as expenses for the current year $ 6,000 and the balance as next year'sexpense.

Chapter 3
Double Entry Method of Accounting

Double entry bookkeeping is the method used to transfer accounting information from the books of prime entry into the nominal ledger. It is the cornerstone of accounts preparation and is surprisingly simple.

Unit 1　Accounting Elements and Accounting Equation

1.1　Accounting Elements

Before the accounting process can begin, the organization must be defined. A business entity could be an individual, association, or other organization that engages in business activities. This definition separates personal from business finances of an owner. A business that is owned by one person is called a proprietorship. The owner of the business is known as the proprietor. Here, we will only discuss proprietorship.

In order to appropriately report the financial performance and position of a business, the financial statements must summarise five key elements: assets, liabilities, owner's equity, expenses and income.

1.1.1　Assets

An asset is a resource controlled by the entity as a result of past events from which future economic benefits are expected to flow to the entity. Examples of assets are:

- land and buildings owned by the business;

Chapter 3 Double Entry Method of Accounting

- plant and machinery;
- office equipment;
- motor vehicles;
- stocks of materials or goods for resale;
- money in a business bank account;
- notes and coins (including 'petty cash').

1.1.2 Liabilities

A liability is an obligation to transfer economic benefit as a result of past transactions or events. Examples of liabilities are:

- money owed to suppliers for goods and services;
- bank loan;
- bank overdraft;
- money owned to the tax authorities.

1.1.3 Owner's Equity

This is the 'residual interest' in a business and represents what is left when the business is wound up, all the assets sold and all the outstanding liabilities paid. It is effectively what is paid back to the owners (shareholders) when the business ceases to trade. Four main types of transactions affect the owner's interest in the entity:

- investment of assets in the entity by owner;
- withdrawal of assets by the owner;
- income derived;
- expenses incurred.

1.1.4 Income

This is the recognition of the inflow of economic benefit to the entity in the reporting period. This can be achieved, for example, by earning sales revenue or though the increase in value of an asset.

Revenue represents income which arises in the course of the ordinary activities of an entity. Revenues are classified into many categories depending on their nature, such as sales revenue, services revenue, consulting fees revenue, commission revenue.

1.1.5 Expenses

This is the recognition of the outflow of economic benefit from an entity in the reporting period. Examples of expenses include:

- the cost of salaries and wages for employees;
- telephone charges and postage costs;
- the rental cost on a building used by the business;
- the interest cost on a bank loan.

1.2 Accounting Equation

The accounting system reflects two basic aspects of a business enterprise: what it owns and what it owes. Liabilities and equity are the source of funds to acquire assets. The financial condition or position of a business is represented by the relationship of assets, liabilities and owner's equity, and is reflected in the following accounting equation.

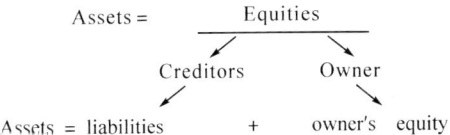

This equation shows assets are equal to equities. Equities are divided into liabilities and owner's equity. The reason why equality is maintained is that the assets controlled by the business which had to be financed by someone, either the owner or lenders. Conversely, the input from the owner and lender has to be represented by asset or assets to the same value. Thus the accounting equation expresses simply that at any point the assets of the business will be equal to its liabilities plus the equity of the business.

Chapter 3 Double Entry Method of Accounting

Example 3.1

The transactions of a new business in its first five days are as follows: Day 1: Avon commences business introducing $1,000 cash.

Day 2: buys a motor car for $400 cash.

Day 3: obtains a $1,000 loan.

Day 4: purchases goods for $300 cash.

Day 5: sells goods for $400 on credit.

Use the accounting equation to illustrate the position of the business at the end of each day (ignore inventory for this example).

Solution:

Day 1: Avon commences business introducing $1,000 cash.

The dual effect of this transaction is:

· the business has $1,000 of cash;

· the business owes the owner $1,000 – this is owner's equity.

Assets	=	liabilities	+	owner's equity
1 000		0		1 000

Day 2: buys a motor car for $400 cash.

The dual effect of this transaction is:

· the business has an asset of $400;

· the business has spent $400 in cash.

Assets	=	liabilities	+	owner's equity
1 000		0		1 000
400 − 400		0		0
1 000		0		1 000

Day 3: obtains a $1,000 loan. The dual effect of this transaction is:

· the business has $1,000 of cash;

· the business owes $1,000 to the bank.

Assets	=	liabilities	+	owner's equity
1 000		0		1 000
1 000		1 000		0
2 000		1 000		1 000

Day 4: purchases goods for $ 300 cash.

The dual effect of this transaction is:

· the business has an expense of $ 300 (expenses reduce the amount due to the owners, in other words, they reduce equity);

· the business has reduced cash by $ 300.

Assets	=	liabilities	+	owner's equity
2 000		1 000		1 000
(300)		0		(300)
1 700		700		1 000

Day 5: sells goods for $ 400 on credit.

The dual effect of this transaction is:

· the business has earned sales revenue of $ 400;

· the business has a new asset to receive payment of $ 400 from their customer.

Assets	=	liabilities	+	owner's equity
1,700		700		1,000
400		0		400
2,100		700		1,400

Unit 2 Double Entry Bookkeeping

Double entry bookkeeping is the method by which a business records financial transactions. It is based on the idea that each transaction has an equal but opposite effect. Every accounting event must be entered in ledger accounts both as a debit

Chapter 3   Double Entry Method of Accounting

and as an equal but opposite credit.

2.1 Debits and Credits

Each account has two sides, a debit side and a credit side. By convention, the debit side is shown on the left and the credit side on the right. For practical purposes, it is both clearer and convenient to think of the words debit and credit as meaning the left-hand and right-hand sides of the page respectively.

Account name (and code)	
Date and reference $	Date and reference $
DEBIT SIDE	CREDIT SIDE

You might see that the account looks a bit like the letter 'T', which is why you might hear manual accounts drawn up in this way referred to as 'T-accounts'.

A recognised shorthand form is used for debit and credit.

Dr = Debit

Cr = Credit

2.2 The Basic Rules of Double Entry Bookkeeping

The basic rule, which must always be observed, is that every financial transaction gives rise to two accounting entries, one a debit and the other a credit. There are five types of account:

- asset;
- liability;
- owner's equity;
- income;
- expense.

Every transaction will affect two accounts because of the dual aspect.

By convention, an increase in an asset or an expense is recorded on the debit (or left-hand) side of that item's account. Assets and expenses are opposites of liabilities, owner's equity and income, so an increase in a liability, owner's equity or income balance should be recorded on the credit (or right-hand) side. It follows that decreases in assets or expenses are recorded on the credit side, while decreases in liabilities, owner's equity or income are recorded on the debit side. If more than one account is used to record a transaction, the total value of the debit entries and the total value of the credit entries for the transaction must be equal.

The following rules of double entry accounting:

- A debit entry will
  - increase an asset
  - decrease a liability
  - increase an expense
- A credit entry will
  - decrease an asset
  - increase a liability
  - increase income

In terms of 'T' accounts:

ASSET			
DEBIT	$	CREDIT	$
Increase		Decrease	

LIABILITY			
DEBIT	$	CREDIT	$
Decrease		Increase	

OWNER'S EQUITY			
DEBIT	$	CREDIT	$
Decrease		Increase	

INCOME			
DEBIT	$	CREDIT	$
Decrease		Increase	

Chapter 3 Double Entry Method of Accounting

	EXPENSE		
DEBIT	$	CREDIT	$
Increase		Decrease	

Unit 3 The Use of Double Entry Bookkeeping

The basic rules of double entry bookkeeping can be illustrated using the following transactions. The date of each transactions is not shown here, but in practice transaction dates would be recorded in the accounts.

3.1 Use of Asset, Liability, and Owner's Equity Accounts

Transaction (a): Ted Andy started a business by investing $ 30,000 in cash.

Cash	Equity of Ted Andy
(a) $ 30,000	(a) $ 30,000

Analysis:

The asset cash and Andy's equity in the business were increased. Since cash isan asset and assets are on the left side of the accounting equation when cash accountwas increased by a debit. Capital of Ted Andy is on the right side of the equationand to show an increase in this account. Therefore, capital of Ted Andy was creditedfor $ 30,000.

Transaction (b): Andy purchased office equipment for $ 2,500 on account.

Office Equipment	Accounts Payable
(b) $ 2,500	(b) $ 2,500

Analysis:

To show an increase in the asset account, office equipment, it was a debit for $ 2 500. Since liabilities are on the right side of the equation, increase to liabilities are shown on the right or credit side of the account. To increase the liabilities of the business, accounts payable was credited for $ 2,500.

Transaction(c): Andy purchased office supplies for cash, $ 350.

Cash		Office Supplies	
(a) $ 30,000	(c) $ 350	(c) $ 350	

Analysis:

One asset was increased while another asset was decreased. There is no change in total asset. Office supplies was debited for the increase and cash was credited for the decrease of $ 350. Office supplies are an asset at the time of purchase even though they will become an expense when used. The procedure used in accounting for supplies will be discussed later.

Transaction (d): Andy paid $ 500 on account to the company from which the office equipment was purchased.

Cash		Accounts Payable	
(a) $ 30,000	(c) $ 350	(d) $ 500	(b) $ 2,500
	(d) $ 500		

Analysis:

The liability accounts payable was decreased with a debit, and the asset cash was decreased with credit for $ 500.

Transaction (e): Purchased office supplies on account, $ 400.

Office Supplies		Accounts Payable	
(c) $ 350		(d) $ 500	(b) $ 2,500
(e) $ 400			(e) $ 400

Chapter 3 Double Entry Method of Accounting

Analysis:

The asset office supplies was increased with a debit. The liability accounts payable was increased with a credit. Asset are on the left or debit side of the accounting equation, and increases to assets are shown on the debit side of the account. Likewise, liabilities are on the right or credit side of equation, and increases to liabilities are shown on the right or credit side of the account.

Transaction (f): Andy withdrew $ 300 for personal use.

Cash		Ted Andy, Drawing
(a) $ 30 000	(c) $ 350	(f) $ 300
	(d) $ 500	
	(f) $ 300	

Analysis:

To decrease the asset account, cash was credited for $ 300. Remember, a separate account, drawing of Ted Andy, is used to accumulate withdrawals by the owner. Therefore, to decrease owner's equity, the drawing account was debited.

3.2 Use of Revenue and Expense Accounts

Revenue and expense accounts are of Ted Andy accumulated increases and decreases to owner's equity. By having a separate account for each type of revenue and expense, a clear record can be kept. Also, revenues and expenses can be kept separate from additional investments and withdrawals by the owner. The relationship of these accounts to owner's equity, and the rules of debit and credit are indicated in the Table 3.1:

Table 3.1

All Owner's Equity Accounts	
Debit to enter	**Credit** to enter
Decreases (−)	Increases (+)

Table 3.1 (continued)

All Expense Accounts		All Revenue Accounts	
Debit to enter	**Credit** to enter	**Debit** to enter	**Credit** to enter
Increases (+)	Decreases (−)	Decreases (−)	Increases (+)

Transaction (g): Received $ 3 500 in cash from a client for professional services rendered.

Cash		Professional Fees
(a) $ 30,000	(c) $ 350	(g) $ 3,500
(g) $ 3,500	(d) $ 500	
	(f) $ 300	

Analysis:

This transaction increased the asset cash, with an equal increase in owner's equity, because of revenue. The asset account cash was debited and the revenue account professional fees was credited. Professional fees is a temporary account that has the overall effect of increasing owner's equity.

Transaction (h): Paid $ 1,000 for office rent for one month.

Cash		Rent Expense
(a) $ 30,000	(c) $ 350	(g) $ 1,000
(g) $ 3,500	(d) $ 500	
	(f) $ 300	
	(h) $ 1,000	

Analysis:

This transaction decreased the asset cash, with an equal decrease in owner's equity because of expense. Rent expense was debited and cash was credited for $ 1 000. Rent expense is a temporary account that has the overall effect of decreasing owner's equity.

Chapter 3 Double Entry Method of Accounting

Transaction (i): Paid bill for telephone service, $ 75.

Cash		Telephone Expense
(a) $ 30,000	(c) $ 350	(h) $ 75
(g) $ 3,500	(d) $ 500	
	(f) $ 300	
	(h) $ 1,000	
	(i) $ 75	

Analysis:

This transaction is identical to the previous one. Telephone expense was debited and cash was Credit for $ 75.

Key Terms

asset	資產
liability	負債
owners' equity	所有者權益
revenue	收入
expense	費用
accounting equation	會計等式
basic accounting elements	基本會計要素
drawing	提款,資本撤回
account	帳户
T-account	T 形帳户
double entry bookkeeping	復式記帳
debit	借方
credit	貸方

Multiple Choice Questions

1. Jackson pays for computer equipment by a cheque from the business bank overdraft. Which parts of the accounting equation are changed by this transaction? (   ).

    A. Assets and Liabilities   B. Assets and Income

    C. Liabilities and Expense   D. Owner's equity and Income

2. Which parts of the accounting equation are affected by paying off a loan by cash? (   ).

    A. Assets, Capital   B. Assets, Liabilities

    C. Capital, Liabilities   D. Assets, Capital, Liabilities

3. What is the purpose of the following journal entry? (   ).

    Dr   Office equipment $ 4 000

      Cr   Purchases $ 4 000

    A. To record the cash purchase of office equipment

    B. To record the credit purchase of office equipment

    C. To correct the error of debiting office equipment to purchases

    D. To correct the error of crediting office equipment to purchases

4. A debit can represent three of the following. Which is the odd one out? (   ).

    A A decrease in an asset   B. An increase in an asset

    C. A decrease in a liability   D. An increase in an expense

5. Which journal entry records a business's payment of $ 1 000 for supplies purchased on account last month? (   ).

    A. Dr   supplies $ 1,000

        Cr   Cash $ 1, 000

    B. Dr   Accounts payable $ 1, 000

		Cr	Cash		$ 1,000
C.	Dr		Cash		$ 1,000
		Cr	Accounts payable		$ 1,000
D.	Dr		Supplies		$ 1,000
		Cr	Accounts payable		$ 1,000

6. Brett Wilkinson, Attorney, began the year with total assets of $ 120,000, liabilities of $ 70,000, and owner's equity of $ 50,000. During the year he earned revenue of $ 110,000 and paid expenses of $ 30,000. He also invested an addi-tional $ 20,000 in the business and withdrew $ 60,000 for living expense. How much is the law firm's equity at year-end? ( ).

A. $ 90,000   B. $ 120,000
C. $ 130,000   D. $ 160,000

7. Andrea started a taxi business by transferring her car which worth $ 5,000 into the business. What are the accounting entries required to record this? ( ).

A.	Dr	Owner's equity		$ 5,000
		Cr	Car	$ 5,000
B.	Dr	Car		$ 5,000
		Cr	Drawings	$ 5,000
C.	Dr	Car		$ 5,000
		Cr	Owner's equity	$ 5,000
D.	Dr	Drawings		$ 5,000
		Cr	Car	$ 5,000

Exercises

1. Answer these questions about two actual companies.

(1) The Gap Co. began the year with total liabilities of $ 1.8 billion and total stockholders' equity of $ 1.6 billion. During the year, total assets increased by

16.6%. How much are total assets at the end of the year?

(2) Johnson & Johnson, famous for Band-Aid and other health-care products, began the year with total assets of $12.2 billion and total liabilities of $6.7 billion. Net income for the year was $2.0 billion, and dividends and other decreases in stockholders' equity totaled $0.4 billion. How much is stockholders' equity at the end of the year?

2. Carl Brown decided to establish an advertising agency to be known as Brownie's advertising. Brown's business transactions for the first month of operations ending June 30, 2016 were as follows:

- Brown invested $40,000 cash in the business.
- Paid office rent for one month, $1,600.
- Purchase office equipment on account, $11,700.
- Paid cash for office supplies, $700.
- Paid telephone bill, $425.
- Received $5,120 for advertising fees earned.
- Paid $4,000 on account.
- Received $3,200 for advertising fees earned.
- Paid $2,200 wages to office secretary.
- Withdrew $5,000 for personal use.

Required:

Journalize the transactions above.

3. Journalize the following transactions for the month of May, 2016. Use the chart of accounts for Excel Appliance Repair Company for account titles.

May 1: Purchase office supplies on account, $500.

May 5: Borrowed $5,000, giving a 90-day, 10% note.May

9: Performed services for $200, which will be paid later.May

10: Owner withdrew $500 cash for personal use.

May 11: Paid the rent, $1,000.

Chapter 3 Double Entry Method of Accounting

May 13: Paid the telephone bill, $ 75.

May 19: Received $ 200 for services previously rendered on May 9. May 2

4: Received $ 1,500 cash for repair services rendered.

May 29: Paid $ 100 to a creditor on account (amount previously owed).

Required:

Enter the transactions into 'T-accounts'.

Chapter 4
Accounting Procedures Ⅰ: Journalizing

Accounting is the process of analyzing, recording, classifying, summarizing, reporting, and interpreting information. Financial data enters the accounting process in the form of transactions (financial events). The flow of information from the initial transaction to the financial statements is illustrated as Figure 4.1.

```
DATA SOURCES
     ↓
BOOKS OF PRIME ENTRY
     ↓
LEDGER ACCOUNTS
     ↓
TRIAL BALANCE
     ↓
FINANCIAL STATEMENTS
```

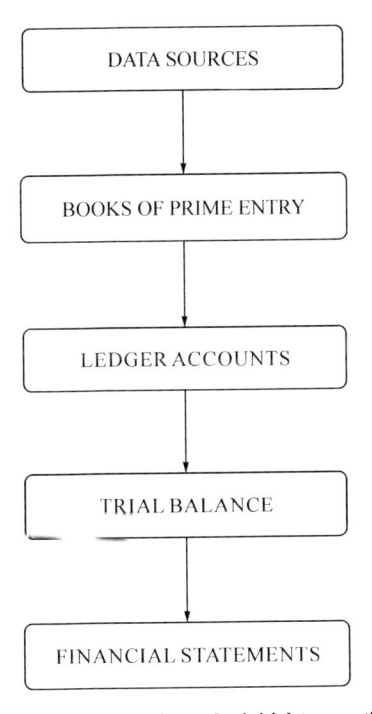

Figure 4.1 The flow of information from the initial transaction to the statements

This chapter will introduce different source documents and books of prime entry which underlie various transactions.

Chapter 4 Accounting Procedures I: Journalizing

Unit 1 Types of Business Documentation

In every business a number of transactions and events will take place every day. The main transactions that take place include sales and purchases (of goods and of services). Others include rental costs, raising finance, repayment of finance, etc. All of these transactions must be adequately captured by the financial reporting system. With most transactions a supporting document will be created to confirm the transaction has taken place, when the transaction took place and the associated value of the transaction. This documentation is vital to the financial accountant, who uses the information on the documents as a data source to initiate the measurement and recording of the transactions.

1.1 Source Documents for Sales

1.1.1 Quotation

A document sent to a customer by a company stating the fixed price that would be charged to produce or deliver goods or services. Quotations tend to be used when businesses do not have a standard listing of prices for products, for example, when the time, materials and skills required for each job vary according to the customer's needs. Quotations can't be changed once they have been accepted by the customer. An example of a quotation is shown as Table 4.1.

Table 4.1   Price List-Quotation

☐Urgent document   ☐Important   ☐General   NO. 20121006

FROM: Yuyuyu Fisheries Services Co. ADDRESS: Guang He Logistics Park Lishui Town, Nanhai District, Foshan City ATTN: TEL: 4000289898 FAX: 075785129262 ZIP CODE:	TO: ADDRESS: ATTN: TEL: FAX: ZIP CODE:

Table 4.1 (continued)

\multicolumn{7}{c	}{SUBJECT：QUOTATION}
\multicolumn{7}{l	}{Dear＊＊Unit, Very grateful to your company's Pro-gaze for our products pro-gaz, We are pleased to quote you our best price with our terms as.}
N	Trade Name	Common Name	Main Ingredient	Effect	Dosage	Price (RMB/kg)
1						
2						
3						

1. Supply cycle：
2. Payment：
3. Delivery：within days after the receipt of your order.
4. Validity：days from the date hereof.
5. Acceptance of the way：site Acceptance.
6. Shelf life：two years.
7. The offer deadline：December 31 2012.
　　Regards！

　　　　　　　　　　　　　　　　　　　　　　　Yuyuyu Fisheries Services Co.
　　　　　　　　　　　　　　　　　　　　　　　Tel：
　　　　　　　　　　　　　　　　　　　　　　　Date：December 31, 2012.

1.1.2　Sales Order

A document of the company that details an order placed by a customer for goods or services. The customer may have sent a purchase order to the company from which the company will then generate a sales order. Sales orders are usually sequentially numbered so that the company can keep track of orders placed by customers.

1.1.3　Goods Dispatched Note

A document of the company that lists the goods which the company has sent out to a customer. The company will keep a record of goods dispatched notes in case of any queries by customers about goods sent. The customer will compare the goods dispatched note that they received to make sure all the items listed have been delivered and are the right specification.

1.1.4　Sales Invoice

When a business sells goods or provides services on credit to a customer, it

Chapter 4 Accounting Procedures I: Journalizing

sends out an invoice. The details on the invoice should match the details on the sales order. It is the evidence and a reminder of the fact that the customer owes the money for the goods or service. When a sales invoice is prepared, it is produced in multiple copies. The top copy or main copy is sent to the customer. The remaining copies remain with the seller. The seller can use these copies for a variety of purposes:

· To update the accounting records (accounts department).

· To file for reference, for example in the event of a query or complaint by the customer (sales department or customer services department).

· To maintain good business and accounting records.

The following example (Table 4.2) of an invoice shows the information that a sales invoice should contain.

Table 4.2

```
                        BLACKHILL FILES
                         742 St Anne's Way
                          York Y05 4NP
                       Telephone: 0190427635
         Invoice No. 23100           VAT Reg. No. 7519516853
                          SALES INVOICE
```

Customer John Forrester Wholesale Supplies Ltd
          Unit 79B
          Oakhampton Industrial Estate
          Bristol BS274JW

Date/Tax Point: 24 June 2016

Order No: E10741

Item No.	Description	Quantity	Item value per unit	Discount	Total $
17340	A5 Lever Arch File	500	$ 2.00	15%	850.00
106912	A4 2 Hole Ring Binder	2,000	$ 1.75	20%	2,800.00
				Sub total	3,650.00
				VAT @ 17.5%	606.81
				Total	$ 4 256.81

Terms: 5% settlement discount for payment within 10 days, otherwise net 30 days

1.1.5 Credit Note

A credit note is effectively reverse of a sales invoice. It is a document sent to a customer stating that they no longer owe money for certain items. A credit note will be required in the following circumstances where an invoice has already been sent out to the customer.

· A customer has returned some or all of the goods because they are damaged or faulty.

· A customer has returned some or all of the goods because they are not the ones ordered by customer.

· A customer has never received the goods although an invoice was sent out.

· An error made on the original invoice is corrected using a credit note.

An example of a credit note is shown as Table 4.3.

Table 4.3

LEWIS.PAPER
47/49 Mill Lane
Manschester M23 6AZ
Telephone: 01618723641
CREDIT NOTE

Credit note No. 21391　　　　　　VAT Reg. No. 4864598220

Customer John Forrester Wholesale Supplies Ltd
　　　Unit 79B
　　　Oakhampton Industrial Estate
　　　Bristol BS 27 4 JW
　　　Date/TaxPoint: 24 June 2014
Original Invoice No. 23120　　　　　　　　　　　　　　Account: 216340

Item No.	Description	Quantity	Item value per unit	Discount	Total $
ST095	A4 Copier Paper Green	20 reams	$ 5.40 per ream	10%	97.20
				Sub total	97.20
				VAT @ 17.5%	17.01
				Credit note total	$ 114.21
Reason for credit note: goods returned as damaged in transit					

Chapter 4   Accounting Procedures I: Journalizing

1.1.6 Debit Note

A debit note is an adjusting document similar to a credit note. It is sent from a supplier to a customer when there is a need to increase the amount owed by the customer. A debit note might be sent out if a customer has been undercharged for goods perhaps because the goods have been charged at a lower price or more goods have been supplied than invoiced.

1.2 Source Documents for Purchases

1.2.1 Purchase Order

A document of the company that details goods or services which the company wishes to purchase from another company. Two copies of a purchase order are often made. One is sent to the company from which the goods or services will be purchased, and another is kept internally so the company can keep track of its orders. Purchase orders are often sequentially numbered. An example of a purchase order is shown as Table 4.4.

Table 4.4   Eurosa Furniture (Kunshan) Co. Ltd

Purchase order   NO.4002401   Date: 2016/05/16

Supplier:	Changlong Wood Industry		Phone:	0435-8752222	
			Fax:	0435-8752567	
No	Item	Description	Units	Quantity	
1	918711	Lola side chair	piece	520	
2	918712	Lola arm chair	piece	260	
3	918780	Lola Bench	piece	180	
Total				960	

1.2.2 Goods Received Note

It is a document of the company that lists the goods that a business has received from a supplier. A goods received note is usually prepared by the business's own warehouse or goods receiving area.

An example of a goods received note is shown as Table 4.5.

Table 4.5

GOODS RECEIVED NOTE				
Supplier: Summerhill Supplies				No. 4621
Supplier DN No.: F3 16				
Date: 20 May 2016				
Time: 10:43 AM				
	Reference	Item delivered	Quantity	Condition
		TL15 wall fittings	11	OK
		PC21 light fittings	4	OK
		MT06 lamp stands	12	OK
				Received in good condition
				signed: P Harman

1.2.3 Purchase Invoice

The supplier usually submits an invoice when the goods or services are delivered, or soon after. The sales invoice issued by the supplier is a purchase invoice to the customer. Whereas a sales invoice represents income, purchase invoices represent expenditure.

1.3 Other Source Documents

1.3.1 Statement of Account

It is a document sent out by a supplier to customer listing the transactions on the customer's account. Including all invoices and credit notes issued, and all payments received from the customer. The statement is useful as it allows the customer to reconcile the amount that they believe they owe the supplier to the amount and the

Chapter 4　Accounting Procedures I: Journalizing

supplier believes they are owed. Any differences can then be queried. A sample of statement of account is given as Table 4.6.

Table 4.6

Viking Paper Limited				
Viking House, 27 High Road, Sheffied S16 6HDE				
STATEMENT OF ACCOUNT			
T Smith & Co.			
(Address)			
Account 31702			
Date	Transaction details	Amount	Balance
		$	$
01/03	Balance, start of March	90.11	90.11
08/03	Invoice – 15021	160.39	250.50
15/03	Invoice – 15100	115.73	366.23
20/03	Payment received	(250.5)	115.73
26/03	Invoice – 15183	66.25	181.93
30/03	Invoice – 15257	228.37	410.35
Amount due at statement date			410.35

1.3.2　Bank statements

Weekly or monthly, a business will receive a bank statement. Bank statements should be used to check that the amount shown as a balance in the cash book agrees with the amount on the bank statement, and that no cash has 'gone missing'.

A bank statement might look something like Table 4.7 shown.

Table 4.7

		Paid out $	Paid in $	Balance $	
	South East Bank plc				
	High Street, Borchester BO1 2ER				
Account No. 22353712					
1 July	Balance b/f			345.00	
8 July	Cheque 23457	100.00		245.00	
18 July	Cheque 23454	278.00		33.00	o/d
20 July	T J Smith		425.00	392.00	
26 July	Cheshire Gas	45.00		347.00	
30 July	Bank charges	56.00		291.00	
31 July	Balance c/f			291.00	

Note: b/f: brought forward; c/f: carried forward; o/d: overdrawn.

1.3.3　Remittance advice

When paying an invoice, some businesses send a remittance advice with their payment. A remittance advice is a document giving details of the invoice that is being paid (or possibly several invoice that are all being paid at the same time), including the supplier's invoice number. This will help the supplier to identify what the payment is for. The following is a typical remittance advice (shown as Table 4.8).

Table 4.8

Supplier name	Account number	Amount paid	Settlement discount taken
		$	$
A C Bryan	1037	265.40	–
Flowers Limited	1002	319.64	16.82
E Patel	1053	396.61	20.87
P Taylor	1025	236.98	–
F Willis	1129	326.89	16.09
Young Fashions	1042	115.79	–
Perry & Co.	1079	163.26	11.12

1.3.4 Receipt

A written statement of an amount of money that has been paid/received. This is usually in respect of cash sales, such as a till receipt from a cash register. The buyer orders goods or services and pays for them immediately or on delivery. The seller delivers the goods or provides the services, and often gives the customer a receipt as evidence of payment.

Unit 2 Books of Prime Entry

In the course of business, source documents are created. The details on these source documents need to be summarised, as otherwise the business might forget to ask for some money, or forget to pay some, or even accidentally pay something twice. It needs to keep records of source documents of transactions, so that it is known as what is going on. Such records are made in books of prime entry.

2.1 Sales Day Book

The sales day book is the book of prime entry for credit sales. The sales day book is used to keep a list of all invoices sent out to customers each day. An extract from a sales day book might look as Table 4.9 shown.

Table 4.9   **Sales Day Book**

Date	Invoice No.	Customer	Total amount invoiced $
06/09/201×	247	GK Kite	105.00
10/09/201×	248	Henn Garage	86.40
15/09/201×	249	Yelson Ltd	31.80
30/09/201×	250	Lynn Prtnrs	1,264.60
			1,487.80

In many businesses, sales consist of a number of different products or ranges of products, or products sold by different departments, or products sold by different geographical regions. Often the managers of a business find it useful to analyse the total credit sales that have been made in these different sales areas. This can be done by analysing the sales according to category or type when they are first recorded, in the sales day book. This will given us an analysed sales day book (Table 4.10).

Table 4.10   **Sales Day Book**

Date	Invoice No.	Customer	Total amount invoiced $	North sales $	South sales $
15/06/201×	68	Louch & Co.	1 370.00	1,370.00	
18/06/201×	69	Framells	1,592.00		1,592.00
30/06/201×	70	Position Ltd	2,376.00	2,376.00	
			5,338.00	3,746.00	1,592.00

The analysis gives the managers of the business useful information which helps them to decide how best to run the business.

2.2 Purchase Day Book

A business also keeps a record in the purchase day book of all the invoices it

Chapter 4　Accounting Procedures I: Journalizing

receives. The purchase day book is the book of prime entry for credit purchases. An extract from a purchase day book might look like as Table 4.11 shown.

Table 4.11　　　　　　　　　**Purchase Day Book**

Date	Supplier	Supplier account number	Purchases $	Rent $	Telephone $
06/06/201×	GK Kite	3011	510.00		
15/06/201×	Yelson Ltd	3012	850.00		
30/06/201×	Lynn Prtnrs	3013		600.00	
30/06/201×	Brit Telecom	3014			351.20
			1,360.00	600.0	351.20

Like the sales day book, the purchase day book analyses the invoices which have been sent in. In this example, two of the invoices related to goods which the business intends to re-sell (called simply 'purchases') and other invoices were for rental and telephone expenses.

2.3　Sales Returns Day Book

When customers return goods for some reason, a credit note is raised. All credit notes are recorded in the sales returns day book. For example, Greg Tyson makes the sales returns (Table 4.12):

Table 4.12　　　　　　　　　**Sales Returns Day Book**

Date	Details	Credit note	Amount
			$
10 July	Charlie	C23	164.50
15 July	Delta	C24	94.00
26 July	Waton & Co.	C25	60.24
			318.74

Where a business has very few sales returns, it may record a credit note as a negative entry in the sales day book.

2.4 Purchase Returns Day Book

A separate day book is used to record supplier credit notes. This is called the purchase returns day book (or returns outwards day book). The purchase returns day book is similar to a sales returns day book. However, it records supplier credit notes received rather than credit notes issued to customers. An example of purchase returns day book is given below(Table 4.13).

Table 4.13   Purchase Returns Day Book

Date	Supplier	Supplier account number	Amount $
05/11	Vast Chemicals	P9704	470.00
10/11	Boxes Co.	P9806	180.00
			650.00

2.5 Cash book

All transactions involving cash at bank are recorded in the cash book. Many businesses have two distinct cash books—a cash payments book and a cash receipts book. It is common for businesses to use a columnar format cash book in order to analyse types of cash payment and receipt.

The following is the cash payments book (Table 4.14) and the cash receipts book (Table 4.15) of a small print business.

Table 4.14   Cash Payments Book

Date	Detail	Total $	Purchase $	Payables $	Rent $
06/06/201×	Cash purchase	1,400.00	1,400.00		
15/06/201×	Accounts payable Mr A	1,600.00		1,600.00	
25/06/201×	Accounts payable Mr B	800.00		800.00	
30/06/201×	Rental	1,000.00			1,000.00
		4,800.00	1,400.00	2,400.00	1,000.00

Chapter 4 Accounting Procedures I: Journalizing

Table 4.15   Cash Receipts Book

Date	Detail	Total	Sales $	Receivables $	Bank interest $
01/06/2016	Cash sales	2,000.00	2,000.00		
18/06/2016	Accounts receivable C Monet	1,500.00		1,500.00	
23/06/2016	Accounts receivable W Gogh	3,000.00		3,000.00	
30/06/2016	Interest Acc #1	100.00			100.00
	Interest Acc #2	60.00			60.00
		6,660.00	2,000.00	4,500.00	160.00

2.6 The Journal

The journal is the record of prime entry for transactions which are not recorded in any of the other books of prime entry. The journal is used to record:

· the correction of errors;

· writing off bad or irrecoverable debts;

· depreciation charge;

· other items not recorded in the other books of prime entry.

An example journal entry for the depreciation charge at end of period is given below (note that the presentation and the narrative explanation of the transaction, which is a requirement for all journal entries):

JOURNAL

14 May   Dr   Depreciation expense

             Cr   Accumulated depreciation

With the depreciation charge for the period

Key Terms

source documents	原始憑證
quotation	報價單
purchase order	採購訂單
sales order	銷售訂單
goods received note	收貨單
goods dispatched note	發貨單
sales invoice	銷售發票
purchase invoice	採購發票
debit note	借記單
credit note	貸記單
statement of account	往來對帳單
bank statement	銀行對帳單
receipt	收據
remittance advice	匯款通知
books of prime entry	原始分錄登記簿
sales day book	銷售登記簿
purchase day book	採購登記簿
sales returns day book	銷售退回登記簿
purchase returns day book	採購退回登記簿
cash book	現金登記簿
the journal	其他業務登記簿

Multiple Choice Questions

1. Which of the following is not a book of prime entry? (   ).

Chapter 4 Accounting Procedures I: Journalizing

  A. Sales invoice   B. Purchase day book

  C. Sales day book   D. The journal

 2. What is the purchase returns day book used to record? (　　).

  A. Suppliers' invoices

  B. Customers' invoices

  C. Details of goods returned to suppliers

  D. Details of goods returned by customers

 3. In which book of prime entry will a business record credit notes received in respect of goods that the business has sent back to its suppliers? (　　).

  A. The sales returns day book

  B. The cash book

  C. The purchase returns day book

  D. The purchase day book

 4. Which document is used to correct an overcharge in an original invoice? (　　).

  A. Credit note   B. Debit note

  C. Dispatch note   D. Goods received note

 5. Which document provides a summary of the credit transactions between a customer and supplier during the previous month? (　　).

  A. Remittance advice   B. Invoice

  C. Statement of account   D. Bank statement

 6. From the following list of situations where an invoice has been sent, choose one that would not require a credit note to be raised: (　　).

  A. a customer has returned some or all of the goods because they are damaged or faulty

  B. a customer has returned some or all of the goods because they are not the ones that were ordered

  C. a customer has never received the goods although an invoice was sent out

D. postage and packaging was omitted on the original invoice

7. Which of the following documents would not be entered in the accounting records after it has been raised? (   ).

    A. A credit note   B. A debit note

    C. A quotation   D. An invoice

Exercises

Explain the purpose of the following source documents, and list them in the order in which they are produced:

- sales invoice;
- purchase order;
- delivery note;
- goods received note;
- purchase invoice;
- sales order.

Chapter 5
Accounting Procedures II: Posting

Unit 1　Ledgers

In most companies each class of transaction, their associated assets, and liabilities are given their own account. For example, there will be separate accounts for sales, purchases, rent, insurance costs, cash assets, inventory assets, liabilities to pay suppliers (payables), amounts due from customers (receivables), etc. There is no rule as to how many accounts a business should have but the system should facilitate effective and efficient accounting and control. Each account in the system is referred to as a 'ledger'.

1.1　Ledger Accounts

In simple terms, the ledger accounts are where the double entry records of all transactions and events are made. They are the principal books or files for recording and totalling monetary transactions by account. A company's financial statements are generated from summary totals in the ledgers.

Ledger accounts summarise all individual transactions listed in the books of prime entry. A business should keep a record of the transaction that it makes, the assets it acquires and liabilities it occurs. When the time comes to prepare an income statement and a statement of financial position, the relevant information can be taken from those records.

The records of transactions, assets and liabilities should be kept in the following ways.

· In chronological order, and dated so that transactions can be related to a particular period of time.

· Built up in cumulative totals.

1.2 The General Ledger

The term 'general ledger' refer to the overall system of ledger accounts within a business. It houses all the separate ledgers required to produce a complete trial balance and, consequently, set of financial statements. It contains details of assets, liabilities, capital, income and expenditure, profit and loss. It also consists of a large number of different accounts, and each account has its own purpose or 'name' and an identity or code. Examples of accounts in the nominal ledger include the following:

· plant and machinery at cost (non-current asset);

· motor vehicles at cost (non-current asset);

· plant and machinery, provision for depreciation (non-current asset);

· motor vehicles, provision for depreciation (non-current asset),

· proprietor's capital (equity);

· inventory-raw material (current assets);

· inventory-finished goods (current assets);

· total trade accounts receivable (current assets);

· total trade accounts payable (current liability);

· wages and salaries (expense item);

· rent and local taxes (expense item);

· advertising expenses (expense item);

· bank charges (expense item);

· telephone expenses (expense item);

· sales (revenue item);

Chapter 5 Accounting Procedures II: Posting

· total cash or bank overdraft (current assets or liability).

When it comes to drawing up the financial statements, the revenue and expense accounts will help to form the income statement, while the asset and liability accounts will go into the statement of financial position.

1.3 The Format of a Ledger Account

There are two sides to a ledger account and an account heading on top, so they are often referred to as 'T-accounts'. The T-accounts is given below:

	Name of account		
Debit side	$	Credit side	$

· On top of the account is its name.
· There is a left hand side, or debit side.
· There is a right hand side, or credit side.

1.4 Balancing Off a Ledger Account

Once the transactions for a period have been recorded, it will be necessary to find the balance on the ledger account:

· Total both side of the T-account and find the larger total.
· Put the larger total in the total box on the debit and credit side.
· Insert a balancing figure to the side of the T account which does not currently add up to the amount in the total box. Call this balancing figure 'balance c/f' (carried forward) or 'balance c/d' (carried down).
· Carry the balance down diagonally and call it 'balance b/f' (brought forward) or 'balance b/d' (brought down).

Example 5.1

Balance off the following account:

Cash

	$		$
Capital	10,000	Purchases	200
Sales	250	Rent	150
		Electricity	75
		Balance c/f	9,825
	10,250		10,250
Balance b/f	9,825		

Unit 2 Control Accounts

A control account is an account in the nominal ledger in which a record is kept of the total value of a number of similar but individual items. Control accounts are used chiefly for trade receivables and payables.

The reasons for having control accounts are as follows:

· They provide a check on the accuracy of entries made in the personal accounts in the receivables ledger and payables ledger.

· The control accounts also assist in the location of errors, where posting to the control accounts are made daily or weekly, or even monthly.

· Where there is a separation of clerical duties, the control account provides an internal check.

· To provide total receivables and payables balances more quickly for producing a trial balance or statement of financial position.

2.1 Receivables Control Account

A receivable control account is an account in which records are kept of transactions involving all receivables in total. The balance on the receivables control account at any time will be the total amount due to the business at that time from its receivables.

2.1.1 Preparing the Control Account

Transactions affecting credit customers are shown as follows:

- sales invoices;
- credit notes for sales returns;
- payments by customers;
- settlement discounts taken by customers (it will be described in a later chapter).

At regular intervals, perhaps weekly or monthly, the total for sales on credit according to the sales day book is recorded as follows:

Dr Receivables control account

　Cr Sales

Immediately afterwards, the individual sales listed in the sales day book are charged to the appropriate personal accounts.

Example 5.2

Greg Tyson is a supplier of widgets. He has three regular credit customers. At the beginning of July, none of these customers owed any money. Transactions with these customers during July were recorded in the books of prime entry. Table 5.1 is sale day book and Table 5.2 is cash receipts book.

Table 5.1　　　　　　　　　　**Sales Day Book**

Date	Invoice No.	Customer	Total amount invoiced
July			$
1	3031	Able	846.00
6	3032	Baker	940.00
8	3033	Charlie	258.50
			2,044.50

Table 5.2   **Cash Receipts Book (extract)**

Date	Detail	Receivables
July		$
20	Able	500.00
25	Baker	390.00
		890.00

The totals of these transactions would be posted to the receivables control account as follows:

```
                    Receivables control account
        $           $
        Sales       2 044.50   Bank                890.00
```

In additional to posting the totals to the receivables control account, the individual transaction details are posted to the personal accounts as follows:

```
                         Able account
        $              $
        Sales Inv      846.00     Bank            500.00
        3031
```

```
                         Baker account
        $              $
        Sales Inv      940.00     Bank            390.00
        3032
```

```
                         Charlie account
        $              $
        Sales Inv      258.50
        3033
```

The ledger accounts can then be balanced and reconciled. The reconciliation of the control account total balance to the total balances of the individual customer accounts is shown below. Table 5. 3 is reconciliation statement.

Receivables control account

	$		$
Sales	2,044.50	Bank	890.00
		Balance c/d	1,154.50
	2,044.50		2,044.50
Balance b/d *	1,154.50		

Note: c/d: carried forward; b/d: brought forward.

Able account

	$		$
Sales Inv 3031	846.00	Bank	500.00
		Balance c/d	346.00
	846.00		846.00
Balance b/d	346.00		

Baker account

	$		$
Sales Inv 3032	940.00	Bank	390.00
		Balance c/d	550.00
	940.00		940.00
Balance b/d	550.00		

Charlie account

	$		$
Sales Inv 3033	258.50	Balance c/d	258.50
	258.50		258.50
Balance b/d	258.50		

Tabel 5.3　　　　　　　　　　**Reconciliation Statement**

	$
Individual customers' balances	
Able	346.00
Baker	550.00
Charlie	<u>258.50</u>
Total of individual account balances	1,154.50
Balance on control account	1,154.50
Discrepancy	<u>0</u>

Here, the total of the individual receivables account balances agrees with the balance on the control account. This should be expected, so there appears to be no error.

2.1.2　Receivables Control Account Reconciliation

For each account, the closing balance is the difference between the total debits and the total credits.

2.2　Payables Control Account

A payables control account is an account in which records are kept of transactions involving all payables in total. The balance on this account at any time will be the total amount owed by the business at that time to its payables.

2.2.1　Preparing the Control Account

Transactions with suppliers are recorded in both the books of prime entry and the payables ledger. The transactions relating to credit purchases from suppliers are:

- purchase invoice;
- credit notes for purchase returns;
- payments to suppliers;
- settlement discounts taken from suppliers (it will be described in a later

chapter).

This information are entered in book of prime entry, and then posted to the payables ledgers as follows:

 Dr Purchase

  Cr payables control account

In additional to posting the totals to the payables ledger, the value of individual transactions is posted to the personal accounts

Example 5.3

Bob James is a car parts distributor. He has four credit suppliers. At the beginning of July, he did not owe any of these suppliers money. Transactions with these suppliers during July were recorded in the books of prime entry as follows (Table 5.4 is purchases day book and Table 5.5 is cash payments book).

Table 5.4   **Purchases Day Book**

Date	Supplier	Supplier account number	Total
July			$
1	Ace	6031	1,692.00
1	Bays	6032	1,880.00
8	Eastern	6033	1,480.50
10	Dans	6034	968.00
			6,020.50

Table 5.5   **Cash Payments Book (extract)**

Date	Detail	Payables
July		$
20	Ace	1,692.00
20	Bays	1,000.00
25	Eastern	1,500.00
		4,192.00

The total of these transactions would be posted to the payables control account as follows:

Payables control account

$	$		
Bank 4,192.00	Purchase		6,020.50

In additional to posting the totals to the control account, the individual transaction details are posted to the personal accounts as follows:

Ace account

$	$		
Bank	1,692.00	Purchase	1,692.00

Bays account

$	$		
Bank	1,000.00	Purchase	1,880.00

Eastern account

$	$		
Bank	1,500.00	Purchase	1,480.50

Dans account

$	$		
Purchase		968.00	

2.2.2 *Payables Control Account Reconciliation*

Reconciliation is very similar to the approach with the receivables control ac-

Chapter 5 Accounting Procedures II: Posting

count. At any time, the balance on the control account should be equal to the total of all the balances on the individual supplier accounts in the payables ledger.

The reconciliation of payables control account is shown below. Table 5.6 is reconciliation statement.

Payables control account

	$		$
Bank	4 192.00	Purchase	6 020.50
Balance c/d	1 828.50		
	6,020.50		6,020.50
		Balance b/d	1,828.50

Ace account

	$		$
Bank	1 692.00	Purchase	1 692.00
	1 692.00		1 692.00

Bays account

	$		$
Bank	1 000.00	Purchase	1 880.00
Balance c/d	880.00		
	1,880.00		1,880.00
Balance b/d		880.00	

Eastern account

	$		$
Bank	1 500.00	Purchase	1 480.50
		Balance c/d	19.50
	1 500.00		1 500.00
Balance b/d		19.50	

Note that there is a debit balance on Eastern's account. This is because Bob James has paid more than the amount of his debt, and Eastern therefore owes money to Bob James. Eatern's account is 'in debit'.

Dans account

	$		$
Balance c/d	968.00	Purchase	968.00
	968.00		968.00
		Balance b/d	968.00

Table 5.6 **Reconciliation Statement**

	$
Individual suppliers' balances	
Ace 0	
Bays 880.00	
Eastern (minus value, because debit balance) (19.50)	
Dans	968.00
Total of individual account balances	1,828.50
Balance on control account	1,828.50
Discrepancy	0

Here, the total of the individual payables account balances agrees with the balance on the control account. This is should be expected, so there appears to be no error.

Key Terms

ledger accounts	帳户
nominal ledger	分類帳
control accounts	控制帳户

Chapter 5　Accounting Procedures II：Posting

receivables control account	應收帳款控制帳戶
payables control account	應付帳款控制帳戶
individual (personal) account	個人帳戶
reconciliation	核對

Multiple Choice Questions

1. The total of the payables control account should equal to the total of：( ).

  A. the sales control account

  B. the individual suppliers' balances

  C. the individual customers' balances

  D. credit purchases

2. Which of the following transactions will not affect the balance of payables control account? ( ).

  A. Purchase invoices

  B. Credit notes for purchase returns

  C. Payments paid to suppliers

  D. Payments received from customers

3. During a period, A Co. has the following transactions on receivables control account. Sales $ 125,000, cash received $ 50,000, sales return $ 2,000. The balance carried forward is $ 95,000. What was the opening balance at the begin-ning of the period? ( ).

  A. $ 22,000 debit B. $ 22,000 credit

  C. $ 18,000 debit D. $ 20,000 debit

4. A business' receivables control account did not agree with the total of the balances on the receivables ledger. An investigation revealed that the sales day book had been overcast by $ 10. What effect will this have on the discrepancy?

( ).

    A. The control account should be credited with $ 10

    B. The control account should be debited with $ 10

    C. The control account should be credited with $ 20

    D. The control account should be debited with $ 20

5. A supplier sends Lord a statement showing a balance outstanding of $ 14,350. Lord's records show a balance outstanding of $ 14,500. The reason for this difference could be that ( ).

    A. the supplier sent an invoice for $ 150 which you have not yet received

    B. the purchase day book has been overcast by $ 150

    C. you have paid the supplier $ 150 which he has not yet accounted for

    D. you have returned goods worth $ 150 which the supplier has not yet accounted for

Exercises

The Porter Emporium is a retailer of household furniture. It purchases goods for resale from four suppliers. The following transactions were recorded in April:

Purchase Day Book

Date	Supplier	Supplier account number	Total
April			$
6	Tango	7801	1,948.00
15	Piper	7802	1,563.00
21	Victor	7803	856.40
28	Romeo	7804	1,065.60
			5,433.00

Chapter 5 Accounting Procedures II: Posting

Purchase Returns Day Book

Date	Supplier	Supplier account number	Total
April			$
10	Tango	7801	487.00
25	Victor	7803	214.10
			701.10

Cash Payments Book (extract)

Date	Detail	Payables
July		$
29	Tango	730.50
29	Piper	1,593.00
29	Victor	642.30
29	Romeo	500.00
		3,465.80

Tasks:

1. Post the transaction totals to the payables control accounts.

2. Post the transactions with individual suppliers to the individual supplier accounts.

3. Draw up and balance the payables control account.

4. Calculate the balance on each supplier account.

5. Reconcile the total balance on the control account with the total of the balances on the individual supplier accounts, and identify any discrepancy.

Chapter 6

Accounting Procedures III: Closing and Adjusting

Unit 1 Trial Balance

Within the general ledger, all transactions are recorded as a debit entry in one account and a credit entry in another account, and the total value of debit entries and credit entries must always be the same. If they are not, something has gone wrong. Trial balance is a long list of all the ledger balances created for a specific date showing the respective debit and credit balances. It is used to check whether the ledger accounts are correct, in so far as the total debit balances and total credit balances are equal.

1.1 The Reason for a Trial Balance

There are three main reasons for preparing a trial balance as follows:

· At the end of the financial year, a trial balance is used as a startingpoint for preparing a income statement for the year and a statement of financial position as at the year end. This is something you will study in the future.

· A trial balance shows the current balances on all the asset, liability, capital, income and expense accounts. This can provide useful information to management.

· In a manual accounting system, preparing a trial balance is a procedure for identifying certain types of errors in the accounts. If the total of debit balances and the total of credit balances are not equal, there must have been a mistake (or sever-

Chapter 6 Accounting Procedures III: Closing and Adjusting

al mistakes) in entering transactions in the ledger accounts. Once the existence of an error has been identified, the next step is to carry out an investigation, and try to find where the double entry mistaken or mistakes have happened. Once the error has been found, it should be corrected.

1.2 Producing a Trial Balance

There are two stages in preparing a trial balance.

Step 1: balance off all the accounts in the general ledger.

Step 2: list all the accounts in the ledger, with their debit or credit balance, and add up the total debit balances and the total credit balances.

1.2.1 Closing off the Ledger Accounts

At the year end, the ledger accounts must be closed off in preparation for the recording of transactions in the next accounting period.

(1) Statement of financial position ledger accounts.

Balancing the account will result in a balance c/f (being the asset/liability/capital at the end of the accounting period) and a balance b/d (being the asset/liability/capital at the start of the next accounting period).

Example 6.1

Balance of the following account:

Bank

	$		$
Capital	10,000	Purchase	200
Sales	250	Rent	150
		Electricity	75
		Balance c/d	9,825
	10,250		10,250
Balance b/d	9,825		

(2) Profit or loss ledger accounts.

At the end of a period, any amounts that relate to that period are transferred out of the income and expenditure accounts into another ledger account called profit or loss.

Example 6.2

Balance of the following account:

Sales

	$		$
Return	500	BankTaken	1,000
to profit or loss	2,000	Receivables	1,500
	2 500		2,500

Profit or loss

	$		$
		Sales	2,000

1.2.2 Preparing a Trial Balance

At the end of the year, once all ledger accounts have been balanced off, the closing balances are summarised on a long list of balances. This is referred to a trial balance. All the closing debit balances are summarised in one column and the closing credit balances in another. Given the nature of the double entry system described in this text the totals of both columns should be agree. If not the discrepancy must be investigated and corrected. The layout of a trial balance is illustrated as Table 6.1.

Chapter 6 Accounting Procedures III: Closing and Adjusting

Table 6.1   Trial Balance as at 31 December 2016

	Dr	Cr
	$	$
Purchases	X	
Non-current assets	X	
Trade receivables	X	
Cash	X	
Share capital		X
Loans		X
Trade payables		X
Profit or loss	X	X
X		X

Example 6.3

Below are the ledger accounts of Lucas as at 31 December 2016. We should balance the accounts, bring down the balances and show all the balances in a trial balance.

Step 1: balance each account and bring down the balances.

Bank

	$		$
Capital	1,000	Purchase	305
Sales	300	Motor car	400
Receivables	100	Payables	200
Loan	600	Rent	40
		Balance c/d	1,055
	2,000		2,000
Balance b/d	1,055		

Capital

	$		$
Balance c/d	1,000	Bank	1,000
	1,000		1,000
		Balance b/d	1,000

Motor car

	$		$
Bank	400	Balance c/d	400
	400		400
Balance b/d	400		

Payables

	$		$
Bank	200	Purchases	400
Balance c/d	200		
	400		400
		Balance b/d	200

Receivables

	$		$
Sales	250	Bank	100
		Balance c/d	150
	250		250
Balance b/d	150		

Loan

	$		$
Balance c/d	600	Bank	600
	600		600
		Balance b/d	600

Chapter 6 Accounting Procedures III: Closing and Adjusting

Purchases

	$		$
Bank	305		
Payables	400	Balance c/d	705
	705		705
Balance b/d	705		

Sales

	$		$
		Bank	300
Profit or loss	550	Receivables	250
	550		550

Rent

	$		$
Bank	40	Profit or loss	40
	40		40

Profit or loss

	$		$
Rent	40	Sales	550

Note that the profit or loss account is not closed off at this stage. The balance of this account will be transferred to the retained earnings account in the adjustment process which will be described in a later chapter.

Step 2: prepare the trial balance showing each of the balances in the ledger accounts.

Table 6.2   Lucas

Trial Balance as at 31 December 2016

	Debit	Credit
	$	$
Bank	1 055	
Capital		1 000
Motor car	400	
Payables		200
Receivables	150	
Loan		600
Purchases	705	
Profit or loss	40	550
	2,350	2,350

Look at Table 6.2, the total debit balances and the total credit balances are the same, $ 2 350. Therefore, it appears that the double entry accounting has been consistently carried out.

Unit 2   Error Correction

Errors will sometimes occur in journalizing and posting transactions. In this section, we describe and illustrate how errors may be discovered and corrected.

Trial balance may help in identifying errors. However not all errors are identifiable by trial balance.

```
            Errors can fall into two categories:
           /                                    \
Identifiable by Trial Balance        Not Identifiable by Trial Balance
Trial Balance imbalance              Trial Balance still balance
```

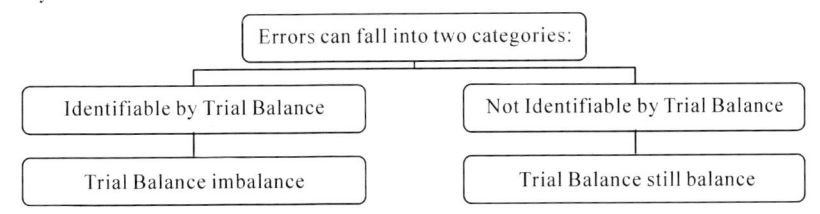

Figure 6.1   Errors are identifiable by frail balance

Chapter 6 Accounting Procedures III: Closing and Adjusting

Figure 6.1 shows that whilst the trial balance provides a useful control mechanism for detecting errors, a balanced trial balance does not guarantee the accuracy of the financial statements.

2.1 Errors Where the Trial Balance Still Balances

The errors which are not disclosed by the trial balance are categorised as follows:

· Error of omission: a transaction has been completely omitted from the accounting records, for example, a cash sale of $ 100 was not recorded.

· Error of commission: a transaction has been recorded in the wrong account, for example, rates expense of $ 500 has been debited to the rent account in error.

· Error of principle: a transaction has conceptually been recorded incorrectly, for example, a non-current asset purchase of $ 1,000 has been debited to the repairexpense account rather than an asset account.

· Compensating error: two different errors have been made which cancel each other out, for example, a rent bill of $ 1,200 has been debited to the rent accountas $ 1,400 and a casting error on the sales account has resulted in sales being over-stated by $ 200.

· Error of original entry: the correct double entry has been made but with the wrong amount, for example, a cash sale of $ 76 has been recorded as $ 67.

· Reversal of entries: the correct amount has been posted to the correct accounts but on the wrong side, for example, a cash sale of $ 200 has been debited to sales and credited to bank.

2.2 Use of Journal Entries for Error Correction

Errors which leave total debits and credits in the ledger accounts in balance can be corrected by using journal entries directly. Otherwise a suspense account has to be opened first (it will be described later), and later cleared by a journal entry.

To remind you, the format of a journal entry as follows:

	Debit	Credit
	$	$
Account to be debited	X	
Account to be credited		X

(narrative to explain the transaction)

Example 6.4

Provide the journal to correct each of the following errors:

(1) A cash sale of $ 100 was not recorded.

| Dr Cash | $ 100 | |
| Cr Sales | | $ 100 |

A transaction previously omitted.

(2) Rates expense of $ 500, paid in cash has been debited to the rent account in error.

| Dr Rates | $ 500 | |
| Cr Rent | | $ 500 |

Correction of an error of commission.

(3) A non-current asset purchase of $ 1 000 on credit has been debited to the repairs expense account rather than an asset account.

| Dr Non-current asset | $ 1,000 | |
| Cr Repairs | | $ 1,000 |

Correction of an error of principle.

(4) A rent bill of $ 1 200 paid in cash has been debited to the rent account as $ 1 400 and a casting error on the sales account has resulted in sales being overstated by $ 200.

| Dr Sales | $ 200 | |

Chapter 6 Accounting Procedures III: Closing and Adjusting

  Cr Rent $ 200

Correction of a compensating error.

(5) A cash sale of $ 76 has been recorded as $ 67.

Dr Cash $ 9

  Cr Sales $ 9

Correction of an error of original entry.

(6) A cash sale of $ 200 has been debited to sales and credited to cash.

Dr Cash $ 400

  Cr Sales $ 400

Correction of an error of reversal entry.

2.3 Errors Where the Trial Balance Does Not Balance

  If the failure of a trial balance to 'balance' is not the result of errors in calculating account balances or preparing the trial balance itself, the error or errors must be somewhere in the accounting records in the ledger accounts.

  The following are examples of errors which could be revealed by a trial balance.

  · Single sided entry-a debit entry has been made but no corresponding credit entry or vice versa. For example, total purchases in the purchases day book are $ 30,760, and this total is posted as $ 30,760 to the purchases account but as $ 37 060 in total to the payables control account. When this type of error happens, total debit and total credits are different, and there will be an imbalance in the trialbalance.

  · Debit and credit entries have been made but at different values. For example, a bookkeeper entered $ 37,543.60 for sales in the sales account instead of en-tering the correct amount of $ 37,453.60. The receivables control account was pos-ted correctly, and so the when total debits and credits on the ledger accounts werecompared, it was found that credits exceeded debits by ($ 37,543.60 − $ 37,453.60) = $ 90.

· Two debit or two credit entries have been posted. For example, sales return from customers are recorded by mistaken with a credit entry in the sales returns account. As a result, the returns would be recorded as follows:

Cr: Sales returns account

Cr: Receivables control account

This type of errors cause an imbalance between total debits and total credits, so the trial balance will not balance.

If there is a difference on the trial balance, then a suspense account is used to make the total debits equal the total credits:

	$	$
Non-current assets	5,000	
Receivables	550	
Inventory	1,000	
Cash	200	
Payables		600
Loan		2,000
Share capital		4,000
Total	6,750	6,600
Suspense account		150
	6,750	6,750

The balance on the suspense account must be cleared before final accounts can be prepared.

2.4 Use of Suspense Account

A suspense account is an account in which debits or credits are held temporarily until sufficient information is available for them to be posted to the correct accounts.

Chapter 6   Accounting Procedures III: Closing and Adjusting

There are two main reasons why suspense accounts may be created:

- On the extraction of a trial balance the details are not equal to the credits and the difference is put to a suspense account.

- When a bookkeeper performing double entry is not sure where to post one side of an entry they may debit or credit a suspense account and leave the entry there until its ultimate destination is clarified.

Example 6.5

On extracting a trial balance, the accountant of ETT found that the credit exceeded the debit by $ 570. She posted this difference to the suspense account and then investigated the situation. She discovered:

(1) The business had purchased $ 2,400 of new equipment, paying by cheque. The payment has been correctly entered in the bank account but has no tbeen posted to any other ledger account.

(2) Purchases on credit of $ 800 have been debited to the payables control account.

(3) Cash sales of $ 1,250 were posted from the cash book to the sales accountas $ 1,520.

(4) The bookkeeper was not able to deal with the receipt of $ 500 from the owner's own bank account, and he made the entry Dr Bank and Cr Suspense.

What journals are required to correct the errors and eliminate the suspense account?

Solution:

The starting position we have is as follows (once we have posted our $ 570):

	Suspense	
	$	$
Trial balance difference	570	

We now need to use journal entries to clear this suspense account. So you need to ask yourself the following questions for each point:

- What should the double entry have been?
- What was the double entry that has been made?
- What is the journal entry we need to correct this?

(1) It should have been: Dr Equipment $ 2,400, Cr Bank $ 2,400.

They have posted: Cr Bank $ 2,400.

correction: Dr Equipment $ 2,400, Cr Suspense $ 2,400.

(2) It should have been: Dr Purchase $ 800, Cr Payables $ 800.

They have posted: Dr Purchase $ 800, Dr Payables $ 800.

correction: Dr Suspense $ 1,600, Cr Payables $ 1,600.

(3) It should have been: Dr Bank $ 1,250, Cr Sales $ 1,250.

They have posted: Dr Bank $ 1,250, Cr Sales $ 1,520.

correction: Dr Sales $ 270, Cr Suspense $ 270.

(4) It should have been: Dr Bank $ 500, Cr Capital $ 500.

They have posted: Dr Bank $ 500, Cr Suspense $ 500.

correction: Dr Suspense $ 500, Cr Capital $ 500.

Now you can post all of the journals that you have listed under the corrections which affect the suspense account.

Then you can balance off your suspense account and it should balance on both the debit and credit sides. Hence, this will clear your suspense account and leave it with a nil balance.

Once you have done so, you should get the following result:

Suspense

	$		$
Trial balance difference	570	Equipment (1)	2 400
Payables (2)	1 600	Sales (3)	270
Capital (4)	500		
	2,670		2,670

Chapter 6 Accounting Procedures III: Closing and Adjusting

Unit 3 Adjustments

As well as adjusting the trial balance figures for any errors identified there are also a number of common adjustments made at the end of the accounting period. These include:

- closing inventory (cost of sales);
- depreciation for the year;
- accruals and prepayments;
- irrecoverable debts and allowances for double debts.

These adjustments need to be processed before the financial statements can be created.

3.1 Cost of Sales

During the journalizing and posting process, you may recognise that the relevant sales and purchases are recorded but the increase and decrease in inventory assets is ignored. The movement in inventory is only considered on an annual basis. In this way a business can calculate exactly how much inventory they have used in the year to calculate cost of sales. Cost of sales is a major expense item for most non-service businesses and is directly related to sales revenue. It includes the cost of all goods sold during the same accounting period in which relative sales are made.

If all purchases are sold during the period (i.e., no closing inventories) then purchases will equals to cost of sales, which is charged in income statement. However, if there are inventories at end, then cost of sales will not equals to the purchases in the period and therefore adjustments below should be made:

- Opening inventories-items of inventories brought forward from previous period, will be included in cost of sales as these goods are available for sale along with purchases during the year.

· Closing inventories-items of inventories counted by the business at end, will be deducted from cost of sales as these goods are held at the period end (i.e., unsold goods).

The proform for calculating cost of sales is illustrated below:

	$
Opening inventory	X
Purchases	X
Less: Closing inventory	(X)
Cost of sales	X

To provide a simple illustration of the effect of this adjustment, a cost of sales T account has been set up. Please look at Figure 6.2.

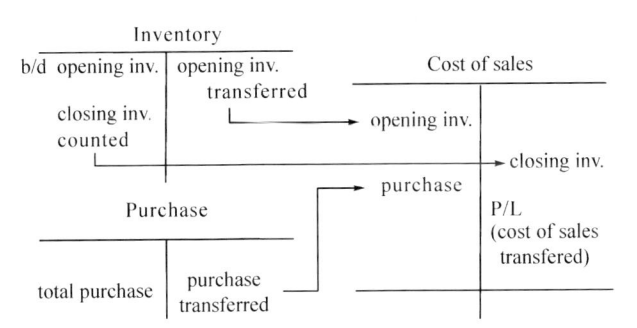

Figure 6.2 A simple illustration

Example 6.6

Peter buys and sells washing machines. He has been trading for many years. On 1 January 2016, his opening inventory is 30 washing machines which cost $ 9,500. He purchased 65 machines in the year amounting to $ 150,000 and on 31 Decem-ber 20 16 he has 25 washing machines left in inventory with a cost of $ 7,500.

Calculate the cost of sales for the year ended 31 December 2016.

Chapter 6 Accounting Procedures III: Closing and Adjusting

	$
Opening inventory	9,500
Purchases	150,000
Less: Closing inventory	(7,500)
Cost of sales	152,000

Inventory

	$		$
b/d	9,500	cost of sales	9,500
cost of sales	7,500		
	7,500	c/d	7,500
b/d	7,500		

Cost of sales

	$		$
inv. (opening)	9,500	inv. (closing)	7,500
purchase	150,000	P/L	152,000
	159,500		159,500

Purchase

	$		$
payables	150,000	cost of sales	150,000

3.2 Depreciation

3.2.1 *Capital and Revenue Expenditure*

A business' expenditure may be classified as one of two types and it shown as Figure 6.3.

```
                        ┌─────────────────┐
                        │   EXPENDITURE   │
                        └─────────────────┘
                    ┌────────────┴────────────┐
```

Capital expenditure	Revenue expenditure
• Expenditure on the acquisition of non-current assets required for use in the business, not for resale. • Expenditure on existing non-current assets aimed at increasing their earning capacity.	• Expenditure on current assets. • Expenditure relating to running the business (such as administration costs). • Expenditure on maintaining the earning capacity of non-current assets. e.g. Repairs and renewals.
Capital expenditure is long-term in nature as the business intends to receive the benefits of the expenditure over a long period of time.	Revenue expenditure relates to the current accounting period and is used to generate revenue in the business.

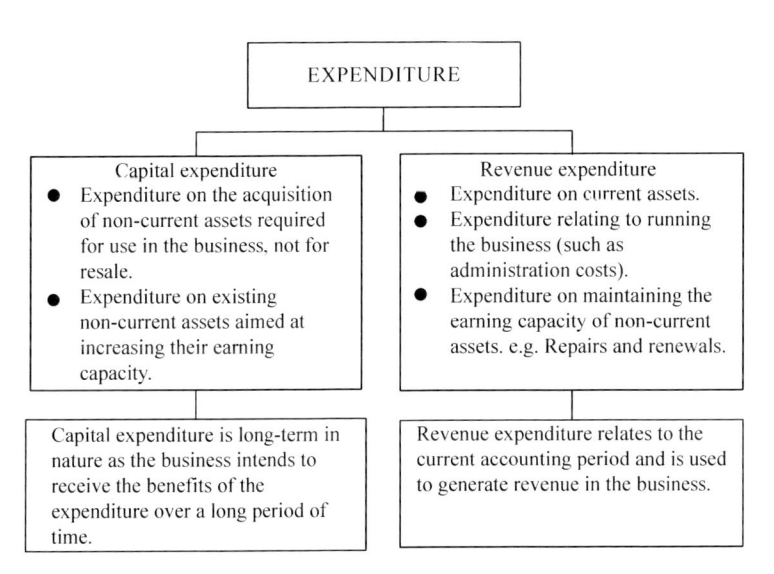

Figure 6.3   Classification of expenditure

3.2.2 *Acquisition of a Non-current Asset*

The cost of a non-current asset is any amount incurred to acquire the asset and bring it into working condition. Table 6.3 shows the category of expenditure.

Table 6.3

Includes	Excludes
Capital expenditure such as: • purchase price • delivery costs • legal fees • subsequent expenditure which enhances the asset • trials and tests	Revenue expenditure such as: • repairs • renewals • repainting • administration • general overheads • training costs • wastage

The correct double entry to record the purchase is:

Dr   Non-current asset

    Cr   Bank/Cash/Payables

A separate cost account should be kept for each category of non-current asset,

Chapter 6　Accounting Procedures III: Closing and Adjusting

such as motor vehicles, fixtures and fittings.

3.2.3　*Depreciation*

Depreciation may arise from:

· use;

· physical wear and tear;

· passing of time (e.g., a ten-year lease on a property);

· obsolescence through technology and market changes (e.g., plant and machinery of a specialised nature);

· depletion (e.g., the extraction of a mineral from a quarry).

The purpose of depreciation is not to show the asset at it current value in the statement of financial position, nor is it intended to provide a fund for the replacement of the asset. It is a simply method of allocating the cost of the asset over the periods estimated to benefit from its use (the useful life).

Land normally has an unlimited life and so does not require depreciation, but buildings should be depreciated. Depreciation of an asset begins when it is available for use.

3.2.4　*Methods of Calculating Depreciation*

(1) Straight-line method.

The straight-line method results in the same charge every year and is used wherever the pattern of usage of an asset is consistent throughout its life. Buildings are commonly depreciated using this method because businesses will commonly get the same usage out of a building every year.

Depreciation charge = (Cost−Residual value) / Useful life

Residual value: the estimated disposal value of the asset at the end of its useful life.

Useful life: the estimated number of years during which the business will use the asset.

For example, Mersley purchase its building for $36,000 on January 22. Because the building was old, its estimated useful life is only 20 years with no residualvalue. Therefore, the building's monthly depreciation expense is $150($36,000cost divided by 240 months).

(2) Reducing balance method.

The reducing balance method results in a constantly reducing depreciation charge throughout the life of the asset. This is used to reflect the expectation that the asset will be used less and less as it ages. This is a common method of depreciation for vehicles, where it is expected that they will provide less service to the business as they age because of the increased need to service/repair them as their mileage increase.

Depreciation charge = X%×carrying value (CV)

CV: original cost of the non-current asset less accumulated depreciation on the asset to date.

Example 6.7

Dev, a trader, purchased an item of plant for $1,000 on August 2016 which he depreciates on the reducing balance at 20% pa. What is the depreciation charge for each of the first five years if the accounting year end at 31 July?

Solution:

Year	Depreciation charge %× CV	Depreciation charge $	cumulative depreciation $
1	20%× $1,000	200	200
2	20%×($1,000−200)	160	360
3	20%×($1,000−360)	128	488
4	20%×($1,000−488)	102	590
5	20%×($1,000−590)	82	672

3. 2. 5 Accounting for Depreciation

Which ever method is used to calculate depreciation, the accounting remains the same:

Dr   Depreciation

　　Cr   Accumulated depreciation

The depreciation expense account is a profit or loss account and therefore is not cumulative. The accumulated depreciation account is a statement of financial position account and as the name suggests is cumulative (i.e., reflects all depreciation to date). On the statement of financial position it is shown as a reduction against the cost of non-current assets:

	$
Cost	X
Accumulated depreciation	(X)
CV	X

3. 3 Accruals and Prepayments

The accruals concept is that income and expenses should be matched together and dealt with in the statement of profit or loss for the period to which they relate, regardless of the period in which the cash was actually received or paid. Therefore, all of the expenses involved in making the sales for a period should be matched with the sales income and dealt with in the period in which the sales themselves are accounted for.

3. 3. 1 Accrued Expenditure

An accrual arises where expenses of the business, relating to the year, have not been paid by the year end.

In this case, it is necessary to record the extra expanse relevant to the year and create a corresponding statement of financial position liability (called an accrual):

 Dr Expense account   X

  Cr Accrual   X

Accrued expenditure will reduce profit in the statement of profit or loss and will also create a current liability on the statement of financial position. For example, if we were to put through an accrual of $500 for telephone expenses. The double entry would like blew:

 Dr Telephone expenses $500

  Cr Accruals $500

The additional telephone expense would reduce profit by $500. The additional accrual would increase current liabilities by $500.

Example 6.8

A business' electricity charges amount to $12,000 pa. In the year to 31 December 2015, $9,000 has been paid. The electricity for the final quarter is paid in January 2016.

What year-end accrual is required and what is the electricity expense for the year?

Show the relevant entries in the ledger accounts.

Solution:

· The total expense charged to the statement of profit or loss in respect of electricity should be $12,000.

· The year-end accrual is the $3,000 expense that has not been paid in cash. The double entry required as follows:

 Dr Electricity expense $3,000

  Cr Accruals $3,000

Chapter 6 Accounting Procedures III: Closing and Adjusting

Electricity expense

	$		$
Cash	9,000	Profit or loss	12,000
Accrual c/f	3,000		
	12,000		12,000
		Accrual b/f	3,000

3.3.2 Prepaid Expenditure

A prepayment arises where some of the following year's expenses have been paid in the current year.

In this case, it is necessary to remove that part of the expense which is not relevant to this year and create a corresponding statement of financial position asset (called a prepayment). The double entry is shown as follows:

Dr Prepayment   X
 Cr Expense account   X

Prepaid expenditure increases profit on the statement of profit or loss and also creates a current asset to be included on the statement of financial position.

For example, if we were to put a prepayment of $ 1,000 in our financial statements for insurance, the double entry would be:

Dr Prepayments $ 1,000
 Cr Insurance expense $ 1,000

The prepayments side would increase our current assets by the $ 1,000. The insurance expense would decrease by the $ 1,000, and hence increase our overall profits.

Example 6.9

The annual insurance charge for a business is $ 24,000 pa. $ 30,000 was paid on 1 January 2016 in respect of future insurance charges.

For the year-ended 31 December 2016 what is the closing prepayment and the insurance expense for the year? Show the relevant entries in the ledger accounts.

Solution:

· The total expense charged to the statement of profit or loss in respect of insurance should be $ 24,000.

· The year-end prepayment is the $ 6,000 that has been paid in respect of 2017.

The double entry required is:

Dr   Prepayment $ 6,000
    Cr   Insurance expense $ 6,000

Insurance expense

	$		$
Cash	30,000	Profit or loss	24,000
		Prepayments c/f	6,000
	30,000		30,000
Prepayments c/f	6,000		

3.3.3 Accrued Income

Accrued income arises where income has been earned in the accounting period but has not yet been received.

In this case, it is necessary to record the extra income in the statement of profit or loss and create a corresponding asset in the statement of financial position (called accrued income). The double entry is shown as follows:

Dr   Accrued income   X
    Cr   Income   X

Accrued income creates an additional current asset on our statement of financial position. It also creates additional income on our statement of position or loss, and hence this will increase overall profits.

Chapter 6 Accounting Procedures III: Closing and Adjusting

Example 6. 10

A business earns bank interest income of $ 300 per month. $ 3,000 bank in-terest income has been received in the year to 31 December 2016.

What is the year-end asset and what is the bank interest income for the year? Show the relevant entries in the ledger accounts.

Solution:

• The total amount credited to the statement of profit or loss in respect of interest should be $ 3,600 (12 × $ 300).

• The year-end accrued income asset is the $ 600 that has not yet been received.

The double entry required as below:

Dr   Accrued income $ 600
    Cr   Bank interest income $ 600

Bank interest income

	$		$
Profit or loss	3 600	Bank	3,000
		Accrued income c/f	600
	3 600		3,600
Accrual income b/f	600		

3. 3. 4 Prepaid Income

Prepaid income arises where income has been received in the accounting period but which relates to the next accounting period.

In this case, it is necessary to remove the income not relating to the year from the statement of profit or loss and create a corresponding liability in the statement of financial position (called prepaid income). The double entry would be:

Dr   Income   X
    Cr   Prepaid income   X

Prepaid income reduces income on the statement of profit or loss and hence reduces overall profits too. It also creates a current liability on our statement of financial position.

Example 6.11

A business rents out a property at an income of $ 4,000 per month, $ 64,000 has been received in the year ended 31 December 2016.

What is the year-end liability and what is the rental income for the year? Show the relevant entries in the ledger accounts.

Solution:

· The total amount credited to the statement of profit or loss in respect of rent should be $ 48,000 (12× $ 4 000).

· The year-end prepaid income liability is the $ 16,000 ($ 64,000 − $ 48,000) that has been received in respect of next year.

The double entry required is:

Dr   Rental income $ 16,000
    Cr   Prepaid income $ 16,000

Rental income

	$		$
Profit or loss	48,000	Cash	64,000
Prepaid income c/f	16,000		
	64,000		64,000
		Prepaid income b/f	16,000

3.4 Irrecoverable Debts and Allowances for Double Debts

The accruals concept dictates that when a sales is made, it is recognised in the accounts, regardless of whether or not the cash has been received. Occasionally customers either refuse to or cannot settle their outstanding debts. If it is highly unlikely that the amount owed by a customer will be received, then this debts is known as an

Chapter 6　Accounting Procedures III: Closing and Adjusting

irrecoverable debt. These are 'written' off by removing them from the ledger accounts completely. An irrecoverable debt could occur when, for example, a customer has gone bankrupt.

If there is concern over whether a customer will pay, but there is still hope that the amount (or at least some of it) can be recovered then an 'allowance' is created. Unlike an irrecoverable, these items are left in the receivables ledger but a separate and opposite account is set up that temporarily offsets the asset. If the balance is eventually paid the allowance can be easily removed.

3.4.1 Accounting for Irrecoverable Debts

An irrecoverable debt is a debt which is, or is considered to be, uncollectable. With such debts it is prudent to remove them from the accounts and to charge the amount as an expense for irrecoverable debts to the statement of profit or loss. The original sale remains in the accounts as this did actually take place.

The double entry required should be:

Dr　Irrecoverable debts expense　　　　　　　　　　X
　Cr　Receivables　　　　　　　　　　　　　　　　　　X

Example 6.12

Araf & Co. have total accounts receivable at the end of their accounting period of $ 45 000. Of these it is discovered that one, Mr Xiun who owes $ 790, has been declared bankrupt, and another who gave his name as Mr Jones has totally dis-appeared owing Araf & Co. $ 1,240.

Calculate the effect in the financial statements of writing off these debts as irrecoverable.

Solution:

As the two debts are considered to be irrecoverable, they must be removed from receivables. The double entry required is as follows:

Dr　Irrecoverable debts expense　　　　　　　　$ 790
　Cr　Receivables-Mr Xiun　　　　　　　　　　　　　$ 790

Dr	Irrecoverable debts expense	$ 1,240
Cr	Receivables-Mr Jones	$ 1,240

Receivables

	$		$
Balance at end	45,000	Irrecoverable debts	
		– Mr Xiun	790
		– Mr Jones	1,240
		Balance c/f	42,970
	45,000		45,000
Balance b/f	42,970		

Irrecoverable debts expense

	$		$
Receivables			
– Mr Xiun	790		
Receivables			
– Mr Jones	1,240	Profit or loss	2,030
	2,030		2,030

Note that the sales revenue account has not been altered and the original sales to Mr Xiun and Mr Jones remain. This is because these sales actually took place and it is only after the sale that the expense of not being able to collect these debts has occurred.

3.4.2 *Accounting for Irrecoverable Debts Recovered*

An irrecoverable debt which has been written off might occasionally be unexpectedly paid. Because the debt has already been written off, it no longer exists in the statement of financial position and so the cash received cannot be offset against it in the usual way. Instead, the cash received is offset against the irrecoverable debts expense.

Chapter 6 Accounting Procedures III: Closing and Adjusting

Regardless of when the payment is received, the double entry required to achieve this is:

Dr   Cash   X
   Cr   Irrecoverable debts expense   X

3.4.3 *Accounting for the Allowance for Receivables*

There may be some debts in the accounts where there is some cause for concern but they are not yet definitely irrecoverable. It is prudent to recognise the possible expense of not collecting the debt in the statement of profit or loss, but the receivable must remain in the accounts in case the customer does in fact pay up.

An allowance is set up which is a credit balance. This is netted off against trade receivables in the statement if financial position to give a net figure for receivables that are probably recoverable. There are two types of allowance that may appear in the organisation's accounts:

• A specific allowance against a specific doubtful debt. The doubtful debt may be a particular invoice or perhaps the whole balance outstanding from a particular customer

• A general allowance against the remaining trade receivables balance.

An allowance for receivables is set up with the following journal:

Dr   Irrecoverable debts expense   X
   Cr   Allowance for receivables   X

If there is already an allowance for receivables in the accounts (opening allowance), only the movement in the allowance is charged to the statement of profit or loss (closing allowance less opening allowance).

When calculating and accounting for a movement in the allowance for receivables, the following steps should be taken:

• Write off irrecoverable debts.

• Calculate the receivables balance as adjusted for the write-offs.

• As certain specific allowance for receivables required.

· Deduct the debt specifically provided for from the receivables balance.

· Multiply the remaining receivables balance by the general allowance percentage to given the general allowance required.

(closing receivables − irrecoverable debts − debts specifically allowance for) × X%

· Add the specific and general allowances required together.

· Compare to the brought forward allowance (opening allowance).

closing allowance−opening allowance

· Account for the change in allowance.

If a higher allowance is required now:

Dr　Irrecoverable debts expense　　　　　　　　　　X

　　Cr　Allowance for receivables　　　　　　　　　　　X

If a lower allowance is needed now than before:

Dr　Allowance for receivables　　　　　　　　　　　X

　　Cr　Irrecoverable debts expense　　　　　　　　　　X

Example 6.13

On 31 December 2014 Jake Williams had receivables of $10,000. From past experience Jake estimated that the equivalent of 3% of these customers were likely never to pay their debts and he therefore wished to make an allowance for this a-mount.

During 2015 Jake made sales on credit totaling $10,000 and received cash from his customers of $94,000. He still considered that the equivalent of 3% of the closing receivables may never pay and should be allowed for.

During 2016 Jake made sales of $95,000 and collected $96,000 from his receivables. At 31 December 2016 Jake still considered that the equivalent of 3% of his receivables should be allowed for.

Calculate the allowance for receivables and the irrecoverable debt expense as well as the closing balance of receivables for each of the years 2014, 2015, 2016.

Chapter 6 Accounting Procedures III: Closing and Adjusting

Solution:

(1) At 31 December 2014:

Closing receivables = 10,000

Allowance required = $ 10,000 × 3% = $ 300

The double entry required is:

Dr Irrecoverable debts expense   300
  Cr Allowance for receivables   300

Allowance for receivables

	$		$
Balance c/d	300	31 Dec 2014	
		Irrecoverable debts	300
	300		300
		Balance b/d	300

Irrecoverable debts expense

	$		$
31 Dec 2014			
Allowance for receivables	300	Profit or loss	300
	300		300

Table 6.4   **Statement of Financial Position Presentation**

	$	$
Current assets		
Receivables	10,000	
Less: Allowance for receivables	(300)	
		9,700

(2) At 31 December 2015:

Closing receivables = 10,000 + 100,000 − 94,000 = 16,000

Allowance required = $ 16,000 × 3% = $ 480

Change in allowance = 480 − 300 = $ 180 (increase)

The double entry required is:

Dr　Irrecoverable debts expense　　　　　　　　　　　　　　180
　　Cr　Allowance for receivables　　　　　　　　　　　　　　　　　180

Allowance for receivables

	$		$
		31 Dec 2015	
		Balance b/d	300
Balance c/d	480	Increase in allowance	180
	480		480
		Balance b/d	480

Irrecoverable debts expense

	$		$
31 Dec 2015			
Allowance for receivables	180	Profit or loss	180
	180		180

Table 6.5　　　　　**Statement of Financial Position Presentation**

	$	$
Current assets		
Receivables	16,000	
Less: Allowance for receivables	(480)	
		15,520

(3) At 31 December 2016:

Closing receivables = 16,000 + 95,000 − 96,000 = 15,000

Chapter 6 Accounting Procedures III: Closing and Adjusting

Allowance required = $ 15,000 × 3% = $ 450

Change in allowance = 450 − 480 = $ −30 (decrease)

The double entry required is:

Dr   Allowance for receivables   30
   Cr   Irrecoverable debts expense   30

Allowance for receivables

	$		$
31 Dec 2016		Balance b/d	480
Decrease in allowance	30		
Balance c/d	450		
	480		480
		Balance b/d	450

Irrecoverable debts expense

	$		$
		31 Dec 2016	
Profit or loss	30	Allowance for receivables	30
	30		30

Table 6.6   **Statement of Financial Position Presentation**

	$	$
Current assets		
Receivables	15,000	
Less: Allowance for receivables	(450)	
		14,550

Key Terms

trial balance	試算平衡
profit or loss	損益
error correction	錯帳更正
suspense account	暫記帳户;懸帳
cost of sales	銷售成本
depreciation	折舊
capital expenditure	資本性支出
revenue expenditure	收益性支出
straight-line method	直線法
reducing balance method	餘額遞減法
accumulated depreciation	累計折舊
accrued expenditure	應計支出
prepaid expenditure	預付支出
accrued income	應計收益
prepaid income	預收帳款
irrecoverable debts	壞帳
irrecoverable debts expense	壞帳損失
allowance for receivables	壞帳準備

Multiple Choice Questions

1. The following are balances in Lim Soon's ledgers at the end of the year.

	$
Sales	21,500

Chapter 6 Accounting Procedures III: Closing and Adjusting

Purchases	8,000
Motor van	11,000
Bank overdraft	4,000
Stock (inventory)	9,500
Capital	3,000

What is the total of each column in Lim Soon's trial balance? ( ).

    A. $ 22, 500   B. $ 28 ,500

    C. $ 31, 500   D. $ 57 ,000

2. The following are the year-end balances in the business ledgers:

	$
Fee income	58, 900
Expenses	21, 200
Receivables	?
Payables	3 ,300
Capital	20 ,000
Bank	24, 500
Office equipment	7, 500

Assuming the trial balance balances, what is the missing figure for receivables? ( ).

    A. $ 29, 000   B. $ 53 ,200

    C. $ 67, 700   D. $ 82 ,200

3. Which of the following is identified by a trial balance? ( ).

    A. A complete reversal of entries

    B. Error of principle

C. Error of single entry

D. Transposition error

4. Which of the following errors requires a suspense account to be opened? (   ).

A. Error in addition of individual supplier account balances

B. Error of commission

C. Cash sale recorded as $ 50, not $ 55 in the sales account and cash book

D. Cash purchases of $ 25 credited to the purchases account and credited in the cash book

5. What must be done with a suspense account before preparing a statement of financial position? (   ).

A. Includes it in assets   B. Clear it to nil

C. Include it in liabilities   D. Write it off to capital

6. Sales returns of $ 460 have inadvertently been posted to the purchase returns, although the correct entry has been made to the accounts receivable control. A suspense account needs to be set up for how much? (   ).

A. $ 460 debit   B. $ 460 credit

C. $ 920 debit   D. $ 920 credit

7. A suspense account was opened when a trial balance failed to agree. The following errors were later discovered.

· A gas bill of $ 420 had been recorded in the gas account as $ 240.

· A discount of $ 50 given to the customer had been credited to discounts received.

· Interest received of $ 70 had been entered in the bank account only.

What was the original balance on the suspense account? (   ).

A. Debit $ 210   B. Credit $ 210

C. Debit $ 160   D. Credit $ 160

Chapter 6 Accounting Procedures III: Closing and Adjusting

8. Which one of the following should be accounted for as capital expenditure?
( ).

   A. The cost of painting a building

   B. The replacement of windows in a building

   C. The purchase of a car by a dealer for re-sale

   D. Legal fees incurred on the purchase of a building

9. Depreciation is best described as ( ).

   A. a means of spreading the payment for non-current assets over a period of years

   B. a decline in the market value of the assets

   C. a means of spreading the net cost of non-current assets over their estimated useful life

   D. a means of estimating the amount of money needed to place the Assets

10. SSG bought a machine for $ 40,000 in January 2016. The machine had an expected useful life of five years and an expected residual value of $ 10,000. The machine was depreciated on the straight-line basis.

   What was the total amount of depreciation charges to the statement of profit or loss over the life of the machine. ( ).

   A. $ 6,000   B. $ 8,000

   B. $ 2,000   D. $ 10,000

11. Which of the following statements is false? ( ).

   A. Accruals decrease profit

   B. Accrued income decreases profit

   C. A prepayment is an asset

   D. An accrual is a liability

12. On 1 May 2016, A Co. pays a rent bill of $ 1,800 for the period to 30 April 2017.

   What is the charge to the statement of profit or loss and the entry in the statement of financial position for the year ended 30 November 2016? (   ).

	Profit or loss	Statement of financial position
A	$ 27, 500	$ 5, 000 in accrued income
B	$ 27, 000	$ 2, 500 in accrued income
C	$ 27, 000	$ 2,500 in prepaid income
D	$ 27, 500	$ 5,000 in prepaid income

13. Details of B Co.'s insurance policy are shown below:

Premium for year ended 31 March 2016 paid April 2015 $ 10, 800

Premium for year ended 31 March 2017 paid April 2016 $ 12,000

What figures should be included in the B Co.'s financial statements for the year ended 30 June 2016? (   ).

	Statement of profit or loss $	statement of financial position $
A.	11, 100	9,000 prepayment
B.	11, 700	9,000 prepayment
C.	11, 100	9, 000 accrual
D.	11, 700	9,000 accrual

14. Vine Co. sublets part of its office accommodation to earn rental income. The rent is received quarterly in advance on 1 January, 1 April, 1 July and 1 October. The annual rent has been $ 24,000 for some years, but it was increased to $ 30,000 from 1 July 2015.

What amounts for rent should appear in Vine Co.'s financial statements for the year ended 31 January 2016? (   ).

Chapter 6   Accounting Procedures III: Closing and Adjusting

	Profit or loss	Statement of financial position
A.	$ 27,500	$ 5,000 in accrued income
B.	$ 27,000	$ 2,500 in accrued income
C.	$ 27,000	$ 2,500 in prepaid income
D.	$ 27,500	$ 5,000 in prepaid income

15. An increase in the allowance for receivables results in: (   ).

　A. an increase in net current assets

　B. a decrease in net current assets

　C. an increase in sales

　D. a decrease in drawings

16. G Co. has been notified that a customer has been declared bankrupt. G Co. had previously made allowance for this receivables.

　Which of the following is the correct double entry? (   ).

	Dr	Cr
A.	Irrecoverable debts account	Receivables ledger control account
B.	Receivables ledger control account	Irrecoverable debts account
C.	Allowance for receivables	Receivables ledger control account
D.	Receivables ledger control account	Allowance for receivables

17. Abacus Co. started the year with total receivables of $ 87,000 and an al-lowance for receivables of $ 2,500.

During the year, two specific debts were written off, one for $ 800 and the other for $ 550. A debt of $ 350 that had been written off as irrecoverable in thepreci ous year was paid during the year. At the year-end, total receivables were $ 90,000 and the allowance for receivables was $ 42,300.

What is the charge to the statement of profit or loss for the year in respect of irrecoverable debts and allowance for receivables? (   ).

    A. $ 800　　　　　　　　　B. $ 1,000

    C. $ 1,150　　　　　　　　D. $ 1,500

Exercises

1. As at 31 December 2014, your business has the following balances on its ledger accounts.

Accounts	Balance
	$
Bank loan	12,000
Cash at bank	11,700
Capital	13,000
Local business taxes	1,880
Trade accounts payable	11,200
Purchases	12,400
Sales	14,600
Sundry payables	1,620
Trade account receivable	12,000
Bank loan interest	1,400
Other expenses	11,020
Vehicles	2,020

You are required to draw up a trial balance.

2. Tubby Wadlow pays the rental expense on his market stall in advance. He starts business on 1 January 2015 and on that date pays $ 1,200 in respect of the first quarter's rent. During his first year of trade he also pays the following amounts:

· 3 March (in respect of the quarter ended 30 June) $ 1,200;

· 14 June (in respect of the quarter ended 30 September) $ 1,200;

Chapter 6　Accounting Procedures III: Closing and Adjusting

· 25 September (in respect of the quarter ended 31 December) $ 1,400;

· 13 December (in respect of the first quarter of 2016) $ 1,400.

Show these transactions in the rental expense account.

3. John Stamp has opening balances at 1 January 2016 on his trade receivables account and allowance for receivables account of $ 68,000 and $ 3,400 respectively. During the year to 31 December 2016 John Stamp makes credit sales of $ 354,000 and receives cash from his receivables of $ 340,000.

At 31 December 2016 John Stamp reviews his receivables listing and acknowledges that he is unlikely ever to receive debts totaling $ 2,000. These should be written off as irrecoverable. Past experience indicates that John should also make an allowance equivalent to 5% of his remaining receivables after writing off the irrecoverable debts.

What is the amount charged to John's statement of profit or loss for irrecoverable debt expense in the year ended 31 December 2016?

What will the effect be of irrecoverable debts on both the statement of profit or loss and the statement of financial position?

Chapter 7
Financial Statements

Accounting statements are the end product of the accounting process, communicating important accounting information to users. The accounting statements, also called financial statements, are the means conveying to the management and the interested outsider a concise picture of the profitability and financial position of a business. The basic financial statements include the statement of financial position, income statement and the statement of cash flows.

Unit 1 Statement of Financial Position

The statement of financial position is a statement of the liabilities, equity and assets of a business at a given moment in time. It is like a 'snapshot' photograph, since it captures on paper a still image, frozen at a single moment in time, of something which is dynamic and continually changing. Typically, a statement of financial position is prepared at the end of accounting period to which the financial statements relate.

1.1 Format of a Statement of Financial Position

A statement of financial position is very similar to the accounting equation. In fact, there are only two differences between a statement of financial position and accounting equation as follows:
- The manner or format in which the liabilities and assets are presented.
- The extra detail which is usually contained in a statement of financial posi-

tion.

Table 7.1 shows an example of statement of financial position.

Table 7.1   Statement of Financial Position for XYZ at 31 December 2016

	$	$
Current assets		
Inventories	X	
Trade and other receivables	X	
Prepayments	X	
Cash	X	
		X
Non-current assets		
Property, plant and equipment	X	
Investments	X	
Intangibles	X	
		X
Total assets		X
Current liabilities		
Trade and other payables	X	
Overdrafts	X	
Tax payable	X	
		X
Non-current liabilities		
Bank loan		X
Equity		
Ordinary share capital	X	
Share premium	X	
Retained earnings	X	
		X
Total equity and liabilities	X	

Note that the suggested statement of financial position format makes a distinction between current and non-current assets and liabilities.

1.2 Current Assets

An asset should be classified as a current asset if it is:

· held primarily for trading purposes;

· expected to be realised within 12 months of the statement of financial position date;

· cash or a cash equivalent (e.g., a short time investment, a 30 day bond).

The main items of current assets are therefore include inventories, receivables, cash, etc.

1.3 Non-current Assets

A non-current asset is an asset acquired for continuing use within the business, with a view to earning income or making profits from its use, either directly or indirectly. It is not acquired for sale to a customer.

· In a manufacturing industry, a production machine is a non-current asset, because it makes goods which are then sold.

· In a service industry, equipment used by employees giving service to customers is a non-current asset (e.g., the equipment used in a garage, furniture in a hotel).

· Less obviously, factory premises, office furniture, computer equipment, company cars, delivery vans or pallets in a warehouse are all non-current assets.

1.4 Current Liabilities

A liability should be classified as a current liability if:

· It is expected to be settled in the normal course of the enterprise's operating cycle.

· It is held primarily for the purpose of being traded.

· It is due to be settled within 12 months of the statement of financial position date.

· The company does not have an unconditional right to defer settlement for at least 12 months after the statement of financial position date.

Examples of current liabilities are:

· loans repayable within one year;

· a bank overdraft, which is usually repayable on demand;

· trade accounts payable;

· tax payable.

1.5 Non-current liabilities

A non-current is a debt which is not payable within the 'short term' (i.e., it will not be liquidated shortly) and so any liability which is not current must be non-current.

Examples of non-current liabilities are as follows:

· Loans which are not repayable for more than one year, such as a bank loan or a loan from an individual to a business.

· A mortgage loan which is a loan specifically secured against a property. (If the business fails to repay the loan, the lender then has 'first claim' on the property and is entitled to repayment from the proceeds of the enforced sale of the property.)

· Loan stock. These are common with limited liability companies. Loan stocks are securities issued by a company at a fixed rate of interest. They are repayable on agreed terms by a specified date in the future. Holders of loan stocks are therefore lenders of money to a company. Their interests, including security for the loan, are protected by the terms of a trust deed.

Unit 2 Income Statement

The income statement is a statement in which revenues and expenditure are matched to arrive at a figure of profit or loss. It shows in detail how the profit (or loss) of a period has arisen.

2.1 Format of an Income Statement

Many businesses try to distinguish between a gross profit earned on trading, and a net profit after other income and expenses. In the first part of the statement, revenue from selling goods is compared with direct costs of acquiring or producing the goods sold to arrive at a gross profit figure. From this, deductions are made in the second half of the statement (which we will call the income and expenses section) in respect of indirect costs and additions for non-trading income.

A sample of the income statement is shown as Table 7.2.

Table 7.2 Income Statement for XYZ at 31 December 2016

	$	$
Sales		X
Cost of sales		(X)
Gross profit		X
Other income		X
Expenses:		
Wages	X	
Rent	X	
Light and heat	X	
		(X)
Net profit		X

Chapter 7 Financial Statements

The two parts of the statement are explained in more detail below.

2.2 Gross Profit

The first part shows the gross profit for the accounting period. Gross profit is the difference between (1) and (2) below.

(1) The value of sales.

(2) The purchase cost of production cost of the goods sold.

> Gross profit = sales-cost of sales

In the retail business, the cost of the goods sold is their purchase cost from the suppliers. In a manufacturing business, the production cost of goods sold is the cost of raw materials in the finished goods, plus the cost of the labour required to make the goods, and often plus an amount of production 'overhead' costs.

2.3 Net Profit

The profit or loss account shows the net profit of the business. The net profit is:
- the gross profit;
- plus any other income from sources other than the sales of goods;
- minus other expenses of the business, not included in the cost of goods sold.

> Net profit = gross profit + non-trading income − expenses

Unit 3 Statement of Cash Flows

The statement of cash flows is a statement reports cash flows during an accounting period. It shows where cash came from and how it was spend. It explains the causes of the change in cash during any given time period.

Whilst a business might be profitable this does not mean they will be able to survive. To achieve this they need cash to be able to pay their debts. If they could not pay their debts they would be put into administration or liquidated. Therefore, the users of the financial statements need to assess the cash position of a business at the end of the year and also how cash has been used and generated by the business during the accounting period.

A statement of cash flows helps to assess:

· Liquidity and solvency — an adequate cash position is essential in the short term both to ensure the survival of the business and to enable debts and dividends to be paid.

· Financial adaptability — will the company be able to take effective action to alter its cash flows in response to any unexpected events?

· Future cash flows — an adequate cash position in the longer term is essential to enable asset replacement, repayment of debt and fund further expansion.

3.1　Format of a Statement of Cash Flows

The cash flow must be presented using standard headings. Note that there are two methods of reconciling cash from operating activities, which will be discussed later in this unit. The following is an example of statement of cash flows.

Table 7.3　**Statement of Cash Flows for the Period Ended 31 December 2016**

	$	$
Cash flows from operating activities		
Cash generated from operations (described later)	X	
Interest paid	(X)	
Income taxes paid	(X)	
Net cash from operating activities		X
Cash flows from investing activities		

Table 7.3 (continued)

Purchase of property, plant and equipment	(X)	
Proceeds of sale of equipment	X	
Interest received	X	
Dividends received	X	
Net cash from investing activities		X
Cash flows from financing activities		
Proceeds of issue of shares	X	
Repayment of loans	(X)	
Dividends paid	(X)	
Net cash from financing activities		X
Net increase in cash and cash equivalents		X
Cash and cash equivalent at beginning of period		X
Cash and cash equivalent at end of period		X

3.2 Cash Generated from Operations

This is perhaps the key part of the statement of cash flows because it shows whether to what extend, companies can generate cash from their operations. It is these operating cash flows which must pay for all cash outflows relating to other activities in the end (e.g., paying loan interest, dividends).

Examples of cash flows from operating activities are shown as follows:
- Cash receipts from the sale of goods and the rendering of services.
- Cash receipts from royalties, fees, commissions and other revenue.
- Cash payments to suppliers for goods and services.
- Cash payments to behalf of employees.

There are two methods of calculating cash from operations—the direct or indirect method. The method used will depend upon the information provided within the question.

3.2.1 Direct Method

This method uses information contained in the ledger accounts of the company to calculate the cash from operations figure as follows:

	$	$
Cash sales		X
Cash received from receivables		X
		X
Less:		
Cash purchases	X	
Cash paid to credit suppliers	X	
Cash expenses	X	
		(X)
Cash generated from operations		X

3.2.2 Indirect Method

This method reconciles between profit before tax (as reported in the income statement) and cash generated from operations as follows:

	$
Profit before tax	X
Finance cost	X
Investment income	(X)
Depreciation charge	X

Loss(profit) on disposal of non-current assets	X/(X)
(increase)/decrease in inventories	(X)/X
(increase)/decrease in receivables	(X)/X
increase/(decrease) in payables	X/(X)
Cash generated from operations	X

This working begins with the profit before tax as shown in the income statement. The remaining figures are the adjustments necessary to convert the profit figure to the cash flow for the period.

3.3 Cash from Investing Activities

The cash flows classified under this heading show the extent of new investment in assets which will generate future profit and cash flows. Examples of cash flows from investing activities are shown as follows:

· Cash payments to acquire property, plant and equipment, intangibles and other non-current assets, including those relating to capitalised development costs and self-constructed property, plant and equipment.

· Cash receipts from sales of property, plant and equipment, intangibles and other non-current assets.

· Cash payments to acquire shares or debentures of other enterprises.

· Cash receipts from sales of shares or debentures of other enterprises.

· Cash advances and loans made to other parties.

· Cash receipts from the repayment of advances and loans made to other parties.

3.4 Cash From Financing Activities

This section of the statement of cash flows shows the share of cash which the enterprise's capital providers have claimed during the period. This is indicator of likely future interest and dividend payments. Examples of cash flows from financing activities are shown as follows:

· Cash proceeds from issuing shares.

· Cash payments to owners to acquire or redeem the enterprise's shares.

· Cash proceeds from issuing debentures, loans, notes, bonds, mortgages and other short or long-term borrowings.

· Cash repayments of amounts borrowed.

Key Terms

financial statement	財務報表
statement of financial position	資產負債表
non-current asset	非流動資產
current asset	流動資產
non-current liability	非流動負債
current liability	流動負債
income statement	利潤表
cost of sales	銷售成本
gross profit	毛利
net profit	淨利潤
statement of cash flows	現金流量表
cash flow	現金流量
operating activity	經營活動
investing activity	投資活動

Chapter 7   Financial Statements

financing activity   融資活動

Multiple Choice Questions

1. The statement of financial position (   ).
    A. shows the financial performance over a period of time and the financial position of the business
    B. tells us the cash flow of the business
    C. summarises the assets, liabilities and equity balances at the end of the accounting period
    D. reports the financial performance of the business over a period of time
2. An income statement shows (   ).
    A. the financial performance and the financial position of the business at a specific date
    B. the cash flow of the business
    C. the financial position of the business at a specific date
    D. the financial performance of the business over a specified period of time
3. The statement of cash flows tells us (   ).
    A. the financial position of the business at a point in time
    B. the forecast cash flows of the business in the future
    C. how much profit the business made during an accounting period
    D. how cash was generated and used during an accounting period
4. Which of the following is NOT an asset? (   ).
    A. Prepayments   B. Accounts receivable
    C. Accrual expense   D. Cash balances
5. Which of the following is NOT a liability? (   ).
    A. Prepayments   B. Accounts payable
    C. Interest payable   D. Accrual expense

6. Company ABC paid $ 18 000 at the beginning of year 2015 in cash for office rental from Jan 2015 to June 2016, how much of the rental should be booked as cost for year 2015? (   ).

  A. $ 9,000   B. $ 12, 000

  C. $ 18, 000   D. $ 24,000

7. Arther had net assets of $ 19,000 at 30 April 2016. During the year to 30 April 2016, he introduced $ 9,800 additional capital into the business and his prof-it for the year was $ 8,000. During the year ended 30 April 2016 he withdrew $ 4,200. What was the balance on Arther's capital account at 1 May 2016? ( ).

  A. $ 5,400   B. $ 13,000

  C. $ 16,600   D. $ 32,600

8. The capital of a business would change as a result of (   ).

  A. a supplier being paid by cheque

  B. raw material being purchased on credit

  C. non-current assets being purchased on credit

  D. wages being paid in cash

9. The following information is available about Andrew's business at 30 September 2016:

	$
Motor van	14,000
Receivables	23,800
Bank balance (a debit on the bank statement)	3,250
Accumulated depreciation	7,000
Payables	31,050
Inventory	12,560
Petty cash	150

| Rent due | 1,200 |
| Allowance for receivables | 1,500 |

What are the correct figure for current liabilities and current assets? (   ).

	Current liabilities	Current assets
	$	$
A.	60,500	35,010
B.	32,250	38,260
C.	57,250	38,260
D.	35,500	35,010

10. Which of the following items would you expect to see included within the operating activities section of a statement of cash flows prepared using the direct method? (   ).

(1) Payments made to suppliers.

(2) Increase of decrease in receivables.

(3) Receipts from customers.

(4) Increase or decrease in inventories.

(5) Increase or decrease in payables.

(6) Finance costs paid.

  A. All   B. (1), (3) and (6)

  C. (1), (2) and (5)   D. (2), (4) and (6)

11. A business had non-current assets with a carrying amount of $50,000 at the start of the financial year. During the year the business sold assets that had cost $4,000 and had been depreciated by $1 500. Depreciation for the year was $9,000. The carrying amount of assets at the end of the financial year was $46,000.

How much cash has been invested in non-current assets during the year?
(   ).

A. $ 4,000   B. $ 7,500

C. $ 9,000   D. $ 10,000

Exercises

1. You are required to prepare a statement of financial position for the Sunken Arches Shoes and Boots Shop as at 31 December 2016, given the information below.

	$
Capital as at 1 January 2016	47,600
Profit for the year to 31 December 2016	8,000
Premises, net book value at 31 December 2016	50,000
Motor vehicles, net book value at 31 December 2016	9,000
Fixtures and fittings, net book value at 31 December 2016	8,000
Non-current loan (mortgage)	25,000
Bank overdraft	2,000
Goods held for resale	16,000
Trade receivables	500
Cash in hand	100
Trade payables	1,200
Taxation payable	3,500
Drawings	4,000
Accrued costs of rent	600
Prepayment of insurance	300

Chapter 7 Financial Statements

2. On 1 June 2016, Jock Heiss commenced trading as an ice cream salesman, using a van which he drove around the streets of his town.

(1) He rented the van at a cost of $ 1,000 for three months. Running expenses for the van averaged $ 300 per month.

(2) He hired a part-time helper at a cost of $ 100 per month.

(3) He borrowed $ 2,000 from his bank, and the interest cost of the loan was $ 25 per month.

(4) His main business was to sell ice cream to customers in the street, but he also did some special catering for business customers, supplying ice creams for office parties. Sales to these customers were usually on credit.

(5) For the three months to 31 August 2016, his total sales were as follows:

· cash sales $ 8,900;

· credit sales $ 1,100.

(6) He purchased his ice cream from a local manufacturer, floors Co.. The cost of purchases in the three months to 31 August 2016 was $ 6,200, and at 31 August he had sold every item. He still owed $ 700 to floor Co. for unpaid purchases on credit.

(7) One of his credit sale customers has gone bankrupt, owing Jock $ 250. Jock has decided to writes off the debt in full, with no prospect of getting any of the money owed.

(8) He used his own home for his office work. Telephone and postage expenses for the three months to 31 August 2016 were $ 150.

(9) During the period he paid himself $ 300 per month.

Required:

Prepare an income statement for the three months 1 June to 31 August 2016.

Chapter 8
Recording Transactions

Business transactions are series of economic activity or event that initiate accounting process. Most transactions can be transacted either in cash or credit. With a cash transactions, payments are either received or paid immediately. Cash is exchanged immediately in order to get the goods or services. With a credit transaction, payments are either received or paid after a pre agreed time frame known as 'credit period'. In this chapter, we will apply what we have learned to go through both the credit transactions and cash transactions.

Unit 1　Recording Credit Transactions

Most transactions between two businesses are credit transactions. A business can purchase goods or non-current assets on credit terms, so that the suppliers would be trade accounts payables until settlement was made in cash. Equally, the business might grant credit terms to its customers who would then be trade accounts receivable of the business.

1.1　Credit Sales

If the sales is on credit terms the customer will pay for the goods/services after receiving them. The credit terms, such as the credit period and the discounts the buyer is allowed, are agreed between the buyer and the supplier in advance.

Chapter 8　Recording Transactions

1.1.1　*Discounts*

(1) Trade discount.

Trade discount are given to try and increase the volume of sales being made by the supplier. By reducing the selling price, buying items in bulk then becomes more attractive. If you are able to source your products cheaper, you can then also sell them to the customers cheaper too.

It is normal policy to show the percentage of trade discount on the face of a sales invoice. For example, if the list price of goods is $ 100 and a 10% trade discount is being given then this might be shown on the invoice as:

	$
List price	100.00
Less: 10% trade discount	10.00
Net price	90.00

From an accounting perspective, trade discounts are deducted at the point of sale. When accounting for a sale that is subject to a trade discount—it is the net amount that should be recorded (i.e., the trade discount does not get recorded separately).

(2) Settlement discount.

This type of discount encourages people to pay for items much quicker. If you pay for the goods within a set time limit, then you will receive a discount. These are often referred to as 'cash discount'. For example, a cash discount of 3% is offered to any customers who pay within 14 days.

If A business give its customer a settlement discount—known as discount allowed, the correct double entries should be:

　　Dr　Discount allowed (expense)

　　　　Cr　Receivables

The expense is shown beneath gross profit in the statement of profit or loss, alongside other expenses of the business.

When a business received a settlement discount from a supplier-known as discount received, the correct double entries are:

Dr Payables

    Cr Discount received (income)

The income is shown beneath gross profit in the statement of profit or loss.

Example 8.1

George owes a supplier, Herbie, $2,000 and is owed $3,400 by a customer, Iris. George offers a cash discount to his customers of 2.5% if they pay within 14 days and Herbie has offered George a cash discount of 3% for payment within ten days.

George pays Herbie with ten days and Iris takes advantage of the cash discount offered to her. The ledger entries required to record these discounts are as follows:

(1) Discount received ($ 2 000× 3% = $ 60).

Dr	Payables	$ 60
	Cr Discount received	$ 60

(2) Discount allowed ($ 3 400× 2.5% = $ 85).

Dr	Discount allowed	$ 85
	Cr Receivables	$ 85

1.1.2 Recording Credit Sales

Credit sales are recorded by increasing account receivables. A company must also maintain a separate account for each customer that tracks how much that customer purchases, has already paid and still owes. This information provides the basis for sending bills to customers and for other business analysis. To maintain this information, companies that extend credit directly to their customers keep a separate account receivable for each one of them. The general ledger continues to have a single accounts receivable account along with the other financial statement account, but a supplementary record is created to maintain a separate account for each customer.

Chapter 8 Recording Transactions

The basic information of credit sales should be entered in a sales day book. The purpose of the sales day book is to make an initial record of all the sales invoices that are sent out to customers.

Example 8.2

Jock Heiss, a sole trader, starts business in September 2016, it makes the following sales in the month (ignore sales tax):

· Sells goods to Forks Ltd (whose sales ledger account reference is S2175) on Sept. 10. The list price of goods is $ 23,500 (invoice number 0968).

· Sells goods to BL Lorries (sales ledger reference S3018) on Sept. 15. The list price of goods is $ 27,000 (invoice number 0969). A trade discount of 3% is being given.

· Sells goods to MA Meters (sales ledger reference S2609) on Sept. 20. The list price of goods is $ 28,600 (invoice number 0970) with a settlement discount of 2% if paid within 14 days.

Jock Heiss recorded the above entries in the sales day book as Table 8.1 shown.

Table 8.1   Sales Day Book

Date	Invoice number	Customer name	Customer reference	Total $
10/09/2016	0968	Forks Ltd	S2175	23,500
15/09/2016	0969	BL Lorries	S3018	26,190
20/09/2016	0970	MA Mesters	S2609	28,600
				78,290

Note that, a trade discount of 3% is given to BL Lorries, therefore the net price of the invoice sent to BL Lorries should be $ 26,190 ($ 27,000×97%). In addition, there is no column for settlement discounts in the sales day book. Although a settlement discount of 2% is offered to MA Mesters when the sales invoice is sent out, it is not known whether the customer will take this discount until the invoice is paid or the discount period has elapsed. Therefore, a settlement discount is recorded only and when the customer decides to take it. Consequently, settlement discounts are recorded in the cash receipts book rather than in the sales day book.

1.1.3 Posting Sales Day Book Totals

From the sales day book, the details have to be transferred (or posted) to the main ledger and enter in the appropriate main accounts, as part of the double entry accounting system. Remember the main ledger is also known as the nominal (general) ledger.

These transaction details are not posted one by one. The entries in the sales day book are totaled and the total figure for credit sales is posted to the main sales account and debtors (receivables) control account in the nominal (general) ledger. Each individual transaction is also posted to the individual memorandum customer accounts.

In order to transfer the total credit sales for a period to the main ledger accounts, the postings should be as follows:

Dr Receivables control
    Cr Sales

Immediately afterwards, the individual sales listed in the sales day book are charged to the appropriate memorandum accounts in the receivables ledger.

Using the example above:

The total of these transactions would be posted as follows:

Dr Receivables control $ 97,690
    Cr Sales $ 97,690

Receivables control account	
$	
Sales 78,290	

Sales account

		$
	Rec. control	78,290

In addition to posting the totals to the nominal (general) ledger, the individual transaction details are posted as follows:

Forks Ltd account

	$	
Sales Inv. 0968	23,500	

BL Lorries account

	$	
Sales Inv. 0969	26,190	

MA Mesters account

	$	
Sales Inv. 0970	28,600	

1.2 Credit Purchase

Most businesses purchase a wide variety of goods and services from suppliers. As a general rule, businesses prefer to buy goods and services on credit. In other words, goods or a services are purchased and usually paid for later.

Purchases, including goods or services, are treated as expenses from an accounting perspective. When expenditure is incurred, a record should be entered in the accounting system. Purchases on credit are recorded in the payables nominal ledger and memorandum accounts.

1.2.1 Recording credit purchase

The first step in accounting for a purchase is to enter its invoice details into a book of prime entry, known as the purchase day book. A purchase day book is similar to a sales day book, but it has a large number of analysis column for every expense account in the nominal (general) ledger.

Example 8.3

Suppose that Jock Heiss occurred following transactions for purchase of goods and services in September 2016:

6 Sept.: purchase goods on credit for which the list price is $ 21,600 (invoice No. 0966) from GJ Kite (supplier account number K06). A trade discount of 3% was received.

15 Sept.: purchase goods on credit for which the list price is $ 24,500 (invoice No. 0945) from Yelson Ltd (supplier account number Y03). The supplier offered a settlement discount of 4% if paid within 14 days.

30 Sept.: received an invoice (No. 2310) for rent from Lynn Prtnrs, costing $ 800 (supplier account number LP02).

30 Sept.: received an invoice (No. 8007) for telephone expense from Brit Telecom, costing $ 268 (supplier account number BT01).

Jock Heiss enter these transactions details in Table 8.2.

Table 8.2 Purchase day book

Date	Invoice No.	Supplier	Supplier account number	Total $	Purchases $	Rent $	Tele. $
06/09/2016	0966	GJ Kite	K06	20,952	20,952		
15/09/2016	0945	Yelson Ltd	Y03	24 500	24,500		
30/09/2016	2310	Lynn Prtnrs	LP02	800		800	

Table 8.2 (continued)

30/09/2016	3007	Brit Telecom	BT01	268			268
				46,520	45,452	800	268

Notice that, the trade discount of 3% offered from GJ Kite will not be recorded in any account. The value of the purchase is the net value shown on the invoice that is $ 20,952 ($ 21,600×97%). It will therefore be this amount that is recorded in the purchase day book.

In addition, there is no column in the purchase day book for settlement discounts received. This is because it is not known with certainty, at the time of purchase, whether the settlement discount will be accepted. When a settlement discount is received, it is recorded in the cash payments book, which is described in a later unit. You will recognise that this is similar to the approach seen earlier for sales.

1.2.2 Posting Purchase Book Totals

Each column of figures in the purchase day book represents an account in the nominal (general) ledger. The total values of the entries in each column are the total amounts invoiced by suppliers, and the total amount of expenditure for each item of expense. These total figures in each column are posted to the nominal (general) ledger as follows:

    Dr   Each expense account

        Cr   Payables control account

As well as needing to know the total amount owed to credit suppliers at any time, shown in the control account, it is also necessary to know exactly how much each individual credit supplier is owed. This is done by the use of memorandum accounts. In the case of suppliers, these are maintained in the payables ledger.

Using the example above:

The total of the purchase book would be posted as follows:

Dr	Purchase	$ 45,452
	Rent	$ 800
	Telephone expense	$ 268
Cr	Payables control	$ 46,520

Payables control account

		$
	Purchase	45,452
	Rent exp.	800
	Telephone exp.	268

Purchase account

	$	
Payables control	45,452	

Rent expense account

	$	
Payables control	800	

Telephone expense account

	$	
Payables control	268	

In addition to posting the totals to the nominal (general) ledger, the individual transaction details are posted to the memorandum accounts in the payables ledger. This is similar to the approach seen earlier for sales.

1.2.3 Cost of Sales

So far you may recognise that during the year the relevant sales and purchases are recorded but the increase and decrease in inventory assets is ignored. The movement in inventory is only considered on an annual basis. In this way a business can calculate exactly how much inventory they have used in the year to calculate cost of sales. Cost of sales is a major expense item for most non-service businesses and is directly related to sales revenue. It includes the cost of all goods sold during the same accounting period in which relative sales are made.

If all purchases are sold during the period (i.e., no closing inventories) then purchases will equals to cost of sales, which is charged in income statement. However, if there are inventories at end, then cost of sales will not equals to the purchases in the period and therefore adjustments below should be made:

· Opening inventories—items of inventories brought forward from previous period, will be included in cost of sales as these goods are available for sale along with purchases during the year.

· Closing inventories—items of inventories counted by the business at end, will be deducted from cost of sales as these goods are held at the period end (i.e., unsold goods).

The proform for calculating cost of sales is illustrated below:

	$
Opening inventory	X
Purchases	X
Less: Closing inventory	(X)
Cost of sales	X

To provide a simple illustration (Figure 8.1) of the effect of this adjustment a cost of sales T account has been set up

```
                        Inventory
        b/d opening inv. | opening inv.              Cost of sales
                         |   transferred
                    closing inv.    └────→ opening inv.
                    counted
                      └─                         └────→ closing inv.
                                         purchase
                      Purchase                    P/L
        ─────────────────────────────             (cost of sales
                                                   transfered)
                    total purchase | purchase
                                   | transferred
```

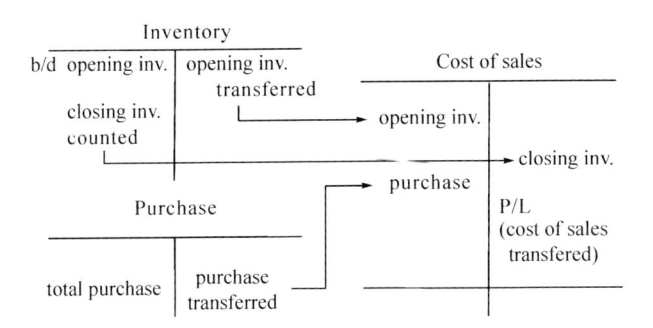

Figure 8.1 Illustration of the adjustment

Example 8.4

Peter buys and sells washing machines. He has been trading for many years. On 1 January 2016, his opening inventory is 30 washing machines which cost $ 9,500. He purchased 65 machines in the year a mounting to $ 150,000 and on 31 December 2016 he has 25 washing machines left in inventory with a cost of $ 7,500.

Calculate the cost of sales for the year ended 31 December 2016.

	$
Opening inventory	9,500
Purchases	150,000
Less: Closing inventory	(7,500)
Cost of sales	152,000

```
              Inventory                              Cost of sales
                $            $                          $              $
   X7  b/d   9 500  cost of sales  9 500      inv.    9,500   inv.              7,500
   Cost of sales  7 500                       (opening)       (closing) purc
              7500    c/d         7 500       hase    150,000   P/L 152,000
   X8  b/d   7 500                                              (cos)
                                              159,500          159,500
              Purchase
                $            $
   payables  150,000  cost of sales  150,000
```

Chapter 8 Recording Transactions

Unit 2 Recording Cash Transactions

The management and control of cash is fundamental importance to any business. When payments are received from customers, a record of receipts has to be made in the accounting system and is the same for payments made by the business.

2.1 Recording Cash Receipts

Business receive money from credit customers who are paying invoices and from customers who do not have a credit account. From an accounting point of view, there is an important difference between receipts from credit customers and receipts from customers without a credit account.

· Receipts from credit customers have to be recorded, not just in the nominal (general) ledger, but also in the individual account of the customer in the receivables ledger, so that the account is kept up to date.

· Receipts from customers without a credit account are treated as cash sales, and both the sales and the receipts have to be recorded in the nominal (general) ledger. These receipts might come through takings in a cash register, or through orders by post, telephone or e-mail, where payment is by cheque or credit card.

When money is received from customers, details of receipts should now be recorded in the accounting system. The first step is to make a record in the cash book, which is a book of prime entry. The cash book is sometimes kept in two separate parts, a cash receipts book for recording receipts and a cash (or cheque) payments book for recording payments.

The purpose of a cash receipts book is to record as follows:
· Receipts from credit customers settling invoices.
· All other receipts, including those for cash sales.

Each payment by a credit customer must be recorded individual. Receipts from cash sales can be recorded as a total. Often the cash book is updated every day, so the cash sales entry is likely to be total cash sales for the day.

Example 8.5

The following amounts were received in September 2016:

6 Sept.: a cash investment from the owner, total $ 20,000.

10 Sept.: rental of $ 1,000 from P Taylor.

16 Sept.: bank loan (short-term) of $ 10,000 from Westpac Bank.

25 Sept.: a cash sale of $ 1,175 from AC Bryan.

28 Sept.: payment of invoice number 0970 by MA Meters (account number S2609) total $ 28 028. A settlement discount of $ 572 was taken by this customer.

30 Sept.: payment of invoice number 0969 by BL Lorries (account numberS3018), total $ 26,190.

Details of receipts above are entered in the cash book as Table 8.3 is shows:

Table 8.3   Cash Receipts Book

Date	Reference	Total $	Debtors (receivables) $	Cash sales $	Other $	Discount allowed $
06/09/2016	Capital	20,000			20,000	
10/09/2016	Rental income	1,000			1,000	
16/09/2016	Bank loan	10,000			10,000	
25/09/2016	Cash sale	1,175		1,175		
28/09/2016	MA Meters, a/c S2609	28,028	28,028			572
30/09/2016	BL Lorries, a/s S3018	26,190	26,190			
		86,393	54,218	1,175	31,000	572

Notice that the final column, for settlement discounts allowed, is a memorandum column. It is used to record any settlement discounts allowed to the customer in return for the early payment of their debt. The settlement discount allowed is recorded in this column as a memorandum item only, because it is not a receipt of cash. It is therefore not included in the total added across. The total is transferred to the discount account in the nominal (general) ledger.

2.2 Recording Cash Payments

Details of cash payments are entered in the cash payments book. The cash payments book is a list of all the payments made out of the business bank account, by cheque and by other methods such as credit card.

There may be a variety of types of payment, other than payments to suppliers, so it is common in an accounting system to find an analysed cash payments book. This is similar to an analysed cash receipts book. In an analysed cash payments book, each payment is recorded on a separate line of the book.

Example 8.6

Jock Heiss makes the following payments in respect of various credit invoices and other items in September 2016:

On 15 Sept., purchase of stock, not on credit, of $ 940 (cheque number 1001).

On 20 Sept., bought a motor car by cheque of $ 4,000, using cheque number10 02.

On 25 Sept., payment of $ 10,000 to GJ Kite (account number K06) in re-spect of an outstanding invoice, by cheque (cheque number 1003).

On 28 Spet., payment of $ 23,520 to Yelson Ltd (account number Y03). Asettlement discount of $ 980 was taken. This was paid by cheque (cheque numb er1004).

On 30 Sept., payment of a salary by cheque of $ 2,500, using cheque number1 005.

Jock Heiss enter these transactions in the cash payments book as Table 8.4 shows:

Table 8.4   Cash payments book

received Date	Reference	Total $	Creditors (payables) $	Purchases $	Salaries $	Motorcar $	Discount received $
15/09/2016	Cash purchase (Cheque 1001)	940		940			
20/09/2016	Motor car (Cheque 1002)	4 000,				4,000	
25/09/2016	GJ Kite (Cheque 1003)	10 000	10 ,000,				
28/09/2016	Yelson Ltd (Cheque 1004)	23, 520	23, 520				980
30/09/2016	Salaries (Cheque 1005)	2 500,			2,500		
		40, 960	33,520	940	2,500	4,000	580

Note that there should also be a column for recording any settlement discount received (taken from suppliers). This is similar to the column in the cash receipts book for settlement discounts allowed. It is a memorandum column only, because it dose not represent a payment of cash from the business bank account. It is needed for posting details of settlement discounts received to the main ledger. An entry should only be appropriate for this column when the payment is made to a supplier.

2.3 Posting Cash Receipts and Payments

The cash book is a book of prime entry, and the next step in recording the receipts and payments is to transfer or 'post' the entries in the cash book to the relevant accounts in the ledgers. The rules for doing this are as follows:

(1) Cash receipts from credit customers.
Dr   Bank
    Cr   Receivables

(2) Cash receipts from owner's investment.
Dr   Bank

Cr   Capital

(3) Cash receipts from cash sales or other cash transactions.

Dr   Bank

　　Cr   Sales/other relevant accounts

(4) Discounts allowed.

Dr   Discount allowed

　　Cr   Receivables

(5) Cash payments made to credit suppliers.

Dr   Payables

　　Cr   Bank

(6) Cash payment made to cash purchase or other expenses.

Dr   Purchase/relevant expenses account

　　Cr   Bank

(7) Discount received.

Dr   Payables

　　Cr   Discount received

Following on from the previous examples, the entries have been made in the cash book should be posted to the ledgers as follows:

(1) Cash receipts.

Receipts from credit customers:

Dr Bank	$ 54,218	
Cr Receivables control		$ 54,218

Receipts from cash sales:

Dr Bank	$ 1,175	
Cr Sales		$ 1,175

Receipts from other cash transactions:

Dr Bank	$ 31,000	
Cr Bank loan		$ 10,000

| Cr Rental income | $ 1,000 |
| Cr Capital | $ 20,000 |

Discount allowed:

| Dr Discount allowed | $ 572 |
| Cr Receivables control | $ 572 |

(2) Cash payments.

Payments to credit suppliers:

| Dr Payables control | $ 33,520 |
| Cr Bank | $ 33,520 |

Payments to cash purchases:

| Dr purchases | $ 940 |
| Cr Bank | $ 940 |

Payments to other cash transactions:

Dr Motor car	$ 4,000
Cr Bank	$ 4,000
Dr Salaries	$ 2,500
Cr Bank	$ 2,500

Discount received:

| Dr Payables control | $ 980 |
| Cr Discount received | $ 980 |

Note that, the details of receipts from individual customers and of discount allowed should also be posted from the cash receipts book to the relevant customer's account in the receivables ledger (this is similar to the process of posting payments to suppliers and discount received from the cash payments book to the payables ledger accounts).

These receipts and payments should be posted to the bank ledger as follows:

Bank

	$		$
Receivables	54 218	Purchase	940
Sales	1,175	Salaries	2,500
Bank loan	10,000	Motor car	4,000
Rental income	1,000	Payables	33,520
Capital	20,000	Bal. c/d	45,433
	86,393		86,393
Bal. b/d	45,433		

Unit 3　Fulfilling an Accounting Cycle

So far, we have followed the transactions of Jock Heiss almost for an accounting period. At the end of the period, financial statements should be prepared after necessary adjusting and closing entries, thus fulfilling an accounting cycle.

3.1　Ledger Accounts Balanced and Closed Off

At each month end, the ledger accounts must be closed off in preparation for the recording of transactions in the next accounting period.

For statement of financial position ledger accounts, the balance on the accounts is carried forward as an opening balance at the start of the new period. A debit balance on an account is shown as an opening balance brought down on the debit side of the account. Similarly, if there is a credit balance on an account, the opening balance brought down at the start of a period should be on the credit side of the account.

Jock Heiss balance off the accounts of assets/liabilities as follows:

Receivables control

	$		$
Receivables	54,218	Purchase	940
Sales	1,175	Salaries	2,500
Bank loan	10,000	Motor car	4,000
Rental income	1,000	Payables	33,520
Capital	20,000	Bal. c/d	45,433
	86,393		86,393
Bal. b/d	45,433		

Bank

	$		$
Sales	78,290	Bank	54,218
		Discount allowed	572
		Bal. c/d	23,500
	78,290		78,290
Bal. b/d	23,500		

Payables control

	$		$
Bank	33,520	Purchase	45,452
Discount received	980	Rent exp.1	800
Bal. c/d	2,020	Tel. exp.	268
	46,520		46,520
		Bal b/d	12,020

Bank loan

	$		$
Bal. c/d	10,000	Bank	10,000
	10,000		10,000
		Bal. b/d	10,000

Motor car

	$		$
Bank	4,000	Bal. c/d	4,000
	4,000		4,000
Bal. b/d	4,000		

Capital

	$		$
Bal. c/d	20,000	Bank	20,000
	20,000		20,000
		Bal. b/d	20,000

For profit or loss ledger accounts, any amounts that relate to that period are transferred out of the income and expenditure accounts into another account called profit or loss.

Jock Heiss close and transfer the income and expenditure accounts as follows:

(1) Transferred the revenue into profit or loss account.

Dr	Sales		79,465
	Rental income		1,000
	Discount received		980
Cr	Profit or loss		81,445

(2) Transferred the expenditures into profit or loss account.

Dr	Profit or loss		4,140
Cr	Salaries		2,500
	Discount allowed		572
	Rent expense		800
	Telephone expense		268

Note that the purchase account is not closed at this stage. It will be closed in the adjusting process later to work out the cost of sales.

3.2 Initial Trial Balance

So far, we have finished all the entries and accounts booking work before the adjusting process for Jock Heiss. We will prepare an initial trial balance to check whether the ledger accounts are correct, in so far as the total debit balances and the total credit balances are equal. It is called an 'initial' trial balance because if the total debits and total credits are not equal, the initial trial balance will have to be corrected. In addition, year end adjustments have to be made and relevant ledger accounts closed off. After that, an 'extended' trial balance is prepared, and is used to prepare financial statements.

Jock Heiss prepare an initial trial balance for September as Table 8.5 shows:

Table 8.5

Jock Heiss

Initial Trial Balance as at 30 September 2016

Account	Debit	Credit
	$	$
Bank	45,433	
Receivables	23,500	
Payables		12,020
Motor car	4,000	
Bank loan		10,000
Capital		20,000
Purchase	46,392	
Profit or loss	4,140	81,445
Total	119,325	119,325

3.3 Preparing Financial Statements

By this stage you should be familiar with the double entry bookkeeping process, closing off ledger accounts and extracting a trial balance. In this section we will explore the adjustments commonly made at the end of the month after the initial trial balance has been drafted and then look at how the financial statements are prepared from this information.

Suppose that Jock Heiss need to made some adjustments for the initial trial balance above. The following additional information as at 30 September 2016 is available:

- Inventory: at 1 September 2016 was nil.

  at 30 September 2016 was $ 3,400.
- Rental of $ 600 was received in advance for next period and salaries of $ 500 was owed at end.
- Motor car is depreciated at 30% annually using the straight-line method.
- An allowance for receivables is to be made amounting to 2% of the outstanding receivables balances at end.

According to the information provided above, the following adjusting entries should be made as follows:

(1) Working out the cost of sales.

Dr Cost of sales		$ 46,392
Cr Purchase		$ 46,392
Dr Inventory (closing)		$ 3,400
Cr Cost of sales		$ 3,400

	$
Opening inventory	nil
Purchases	46,392
Less: Closing inventory	(3,400)
Cost of sales	42,992

(2) Adjusting for rental income and salaries.

Dr Rental income	$ 600
Cr prepaid income	$ 600
Dr Salaries	$ 500
Cr Accrued expense	$ 500

(3) Charging the depreciation for motor car.

Depreciation for the month = 4 000× 30% ÷ 12 = 100

Dr Depreciation expense	$ 100
Cr Accumulated depreciation	$ 100

(4) Setting up an allowance for receivables.

Allowance for receivables = 23 500× 2% = $ 470

Dr Irrecoverable debts expense	$ 470
Cr Allowance for receivables	$ 470

After the adjustments, related profit or loss ledger accounts are closed off again. And then the total balance in the profit or loss accounts is closed to the retained earnings account.

Dr Profit or loss	$ 44,662
Cr Cost of sales	$ 42,992
Rental income	$ 600
Salaries	$ 500
Depreciation expense	$ 100
Irrecoverable debts expense	$ 470
Dr Profit or loss	$ 32,643
Cr Retained earnings	$ 32,643

Before the preparation of financial statements, an 'extended' trial balance is prepared (Table 8.6):

Chapter 8   Recording Transactions

Table 8.6

Jock Heiss

Trial Balance as at 30 September 2016

Account	Debit	Credit
	$	$
Bank	45,433	
Receivables	23,500	
Payables		12,020
Motor car	4,000	
Bank loan		10,000
Allowance for receivables	(470)	
Inventory (closing)	3,400	
Accumulated depreciation	(100)	
Prepaid income		600
Accrued exp.		500
Capital		20,000
Retained earnings	—	32,643
Total	75,763	75,763

Finally, the financial statements are prepared from the information above (ignore income tax).

Table 8.7

Jock Heiss

Income Statement for the Period Ended 30 September 2016

	$	$
Sales		79,465
Cost of sale		(42,992)
Gross profit		36,473
Other income – discount received		980
– rental income (W1)		400
		37,853
Expenses:		
Discount allowed	572	

Table 8.7 (continued)

Rent expense	800	
Salaries (W2)	3,000	
Telephone expense	268	
Irrecoverable debts expense	470	
Depreciation expense	100	
		(5,210)
Net profit		32,643

Workings:

(W1) Rental income

	$
Cash receipts from rental	1,000
Rental prepaid for next period	(600)
	400

(W2) Salaries expense

Cash paid to employees	2,500
Salaries accrued at end	500
	3,000

Table 8.8 Jock Heiss

Statement of Financial Position for the Period Ended 30 September 2016

	$	$
Current assets		
Bank	45,433	
Inventory	3,400	
Receivables	23,500	
Allowance for receivables	(470)	
		71,863
Non-current assets		
Motor car	4,000	
Accumulated depreciation	(100)	

Table 8.8 (continued)

		3,900
		<u>75,763</u>
Current liabilities		
Payables	12,020	
Bank loan	10,000	
Prepaid income	600	
Accrued expense	<u>500</u>	
		23,120
Equity		
Capital	20,000	
Retained earnings	<u>32,643</u>	
		<u>52,643</u>
		<u>75,763</u>

Table 8.9

Jock Heiss
Statement of Cash Flows for the Period Ended 30 September 2016
(using the direct method)

	$	$
Cash flows from operating activities		
Cash receipts from customers (W1)	55,393	
Less: Cash paid to suppliers (W2)	(34,460)	
Cash paid to employees (W3)	<u>(2,500)</u>	
Net cash from operation activities		18,433
Cash flows from investing activities		
Purchase of non-current assets	(4,000)	
Proceeds from rental	<u>1,000</u>	
Net cash from investing activities		3,000
Cash flows from financing activities		
Proceeds from investors	20,000	
Proceeds from short-term loan	<u>10,000</u>	

Table 8.9 (continued)

Net cash from investing activities	30,000
Net increase in cash and cash equivalent	45,433
Cash and cash equivalent at beginning of period	0
Cash and cash equivalent at end of period	45,433

Workings:

(W1) Cash receipts from customers (see cash receipts book)

	$
Cash receipts from MA Meters	28,028
Cash receipts from BL Lorries	26,190
Cash receipts from cash sales	1,175
	55,393

(W2) Cash paid to suppliers (see cash payments book)

	$
Cash paid to cash purchase	940
Cash paid to GJ Kite	10,000
Cash paid to Yelson Ltd	23,520
	34,460

(W3) Cash paid to employees

	$
Salaries expense for the month	3,000
Salaries expense accrued at end	(500)
	2,500

Chapter 8   Recording Transactions

Key Terms

credit transactions	賒銷業務
credit sales	賒銷
credit purchase	賒購
cash transactions	現金業務
cash receipts	現金收入
cash payments	現金支出
trade discount	商業折扣
settlement (cash) discount	結算(現金)折扣
discount allowed	給出折扣
discount received	取得折扣

Multiple Choice Questions

1. Which one of the following is the correct posting from the sales day book?
(   ).

    A. Dr   Sales account   Cr   Receivables account

    B. Dr   Sales account   Cr   Cash account

    C. Dr   Receivables account   Cr   Sales account

    D. Dr   Cash account   Cr   Sales account

2. Jacobs provides its customers with individual trade discounts from list price and a general 2% cash discount on all invoices settled within 7 days of issue. One customer, Caspian negotiates a 20% trade discount. Her transactions during March are:

March 12   Purchases goods with a $ 2,000 list pric

e.March 16   Pays half of the balance on her account.

How much does Caspian owe Jacobs at the end of March? (   ).

A. $ 600 B. $ 640

C. $ 800 D. $ 1,000

3. From the following information, calculate the value of purchases: (   ).

	$
Opening payables	142,600
Cash paid	542,300
Discount received	13,200
Closing payables	137,800

A. 533,900 B. 550,700

C. 609,500 D. 563,900

4. You are given the following information:

	$
Receivables at 1 January 2016	10,000
Receivables at 31 December 2016	9,000
Total receipts during 2016 (including cash sales of $ 5 000)	85,000

What was the sales revenue figure for 2016? (   ).

A. $ 66,000 B. $ 79,000

C. $ 84,000 D. $ 76,000

5. Which of the following statements is correct? (   ).

A. Discount allowed and discount received are both accounted for as an expense in the income statement

B. Discount allowed and discount received are both accounted for as income in the income statement

C. Discount allowed is treated as an expense and discount received is treated as income in the income statement

D. Discount allowed is treated as income and discount received is treated as an expense in the income statement

6. Peter buys and sells washing machines. He has been trading for many years. On 1 January 2016, his opening inventory is 30 washing machines which cost $ 9 500. He purchased 65 machines in the year amounting to $ 150 000 and on 31 December 2016 he has 25 washing machines left in inventory with a cost of $ 7 500.

What was the cost of sales for the year? (   ).

A. $ 150, 000   B. $ 152 ,000

C. $ 159 ,500   D. $ 9, 500

7. Which of the following is the correct posting to record a cash purchase of $ 600 from Georgio Caterers? (   ).

A. Dr   Purchases $ 600;   Cr   Georgio Caterers $ 600

B. Dr   Georgio Caterers $ 600;   Cr   Purchases $ 600

C. Dr   Purchases $ 600;   Cr   Cash $ 600

D. Dr   Cash $ 600;   Cr   Purchases $ 600

8. The total of the discounts received in the cash book is $ 80. How should this be posted in the ledger? (   ).

A. Dr   Discount allowed   B. Cr   Discount allowed

C. Dr   Discount received   D. Cr   Discount received

9. What is the book of prime entry for cash sales? (   ).

A. Cash book   B. Journal

C. Sales day book   D. Sales ledger

10. The following information relates to Minnie's hairdressing business in the year ended 31 August 2016:

$

Expenses	7,100
Opening inventory	1,500
Closing inventory	900
Purchases	12,950
Gross profit	12,125

What is the sales figure for the business? (   ).

  A. $ 32, 775   B. $ 25, 625

  C. $ 25, 675   D. $ 25, 750

11. Kaplin publish study materials and runs courses for students studying for professional accountancy examinations. Details of two transactions that occurred in December 2016 were as follows:

 · Ten students enrolled on a course due to commence in January 2017 at a price of $ 1 000 per student and paid their fees in advance.

 · Kaplin sold study materials to forty self-study students at a price of $ 400 per student who will receive no further support with their studies.

What sales revenue should Kaplin recognise in the financial statements for the year ended 31 December 2016? (   ).

  A. $ 16, 000 B. $ 10, 000

  C. $ 26, 000 D. Nil

12. Vostok sells computer games and is the sole distributor of a new game 'Avalanche'. Customer demand for the new game has resulted in lots of advance orders pending release of the game later in the year. As at 31 July 2016, Vostok had re-ceived customer orders and deposits received amounting to $ 500,000. Vostok an-ticipates that all orders will be despatched to customers by 1 December 2016.

What sales revenue can Vostok recognise in the financial statements for the year ended 31 July 2016? (   ).

A. $ 500,000   B. Nil

C. $ 250,000   D. $ 300,000

Exercises

The trial balance of Kevin Suri (sole trader) as at 31 December 2016 is as follows:

Credit	Account	Debit
$	$	$
	Sales	365,200
	Purchase	266,800
	Inventory at 1 January 20X5	23,340
	Wages	46,160
	Rent	13,000
	Irrecoverable debts	120
588	Allowance for receivables	
	Lights and heat	3 074
	Receivables	17,200
18,568	Payables	
	Bank	3 542
	Buildings – cost	200,000
90,000	Aggregate depreciation	
	Fixtures and fittings – cost	28,000
16,800	Accumulated depreciation	
100,000	Capital	
10,080	Retained earnings	—
601,236	Total	601,236

You are given the following additional information:

(1) Inventory at 31 December 2016 was $25,680.

(2) Rent was prepaid by $1,000 and light and heat owed was $460 at 31 December 2016.

(3) Kevin wishes to maintain the allowance for receivables at 3% of the year end balance.

(4) Depreciation is to be provided as follows:

· building-2% annually, straight-line

· fixtures and fittings-straight-line method, assuming a useful economic life of five years with no residual value.

Requirement:

Prepare an income statement and a statement of financial position for the year ended 31 December 2016.

國家圖書館出版品預行編目(CIP)資料

會計英語/ 陽春暉 主編. -- 初版.
-- 臺北市 : 崧燁文化,2018.07
　面 ；　公分
ISBN 978-957-681-299-6(平裝)
1.商業英文 2.讀本
805.18　　　　107010900

書名：會計英語
作者：陽春暉 主編
發行人：黃振庭
出版者：崧燁文化事業有限公司
發行者：崧燁文化事業有限公司
E-mail：sonbookservice@gmail.com
粉絲頁　　　　　網址：
地址：台北市中正區重慶南路一段六十一號八樓815室
8F.-815, No.61, Sec. 1, Chongqing S. Rd., Zhongzheng Dist., Taipei City 100, Taiwan (R.O.C.)
電　話：(02)2370-3310 傳　真：(02) 2370-3210
總經銷：紅螞蟻圖書有限公司
地址：台北市內湖區舊宗路二段 121 巷 19 號
電話:02-2795-3656 傳真:02-2795-4100 網址：
印　刷：京峯彩色印刷有限公司（京峰數位）

　　本書版權為西南財經大學出版社所有授權崧博出版事業股份有限公司獨家發行電子書繁體字版。若有其他相關權利需授權請與西南財經大學出版社聯繫，經本公司授權後方得行使相關權利。

定價：300 元
發行日期：2018 年 7 月第一版
◎ 本書以POD印製發行